PHOENIX

SHADOW OF THE DOMINION, BOOK 5

BLAZE WARD

KNOTTED ROAD PRESS

Phoenix
Shadow of the Dominion: Book 5
Blaze Ward
Copyright © 2020 Blaze Ward
All rights reserved
Published by Knotted Road Press
www.KnottedRoadPress.com

ISBN: 978-1-64470-092-1

Cover art:

ID 30317359 © Philcold | Dreamstime.com

Cover and interior design
copyright © 2020 Knotted Road Press

Never miss a release!
If you'd like to be notified of new releases, sign up for my newsletter.

I will never spam you, or use your email for nefarious purposes. You can also unsubscribe at any time.

http://www.blazeward.com/newsletter/

Shadow of the Dominion

Longshot Hypothesis

Hard Bargain

Outermost

Dominion-427

Phoenix

Princess Rualoh

The Jessica Keller Chronicles

Auberon

Queen of the Pirates

Last of the Immortals

Goddess of War

Flight of the Blackbird

The Red Admiral

St. Legier

Winterhome

Petron

CS-405

Queen Anne's Revenge

Packmule

Persephone

Additional Alexandria Station Stories

The Story Road

Siren

Two Bottles of Wine with a War God

The Science Officer Series

The Science Officer

The Mind Field

The Gilded Cage

The Pleasure Dome

The Doomsday Vault

The Last Flagship

The Hammerfield Gambit

The Hammerfield Payoff

Earth Force Sky Patrol

Birth of the Star Dragon

Flight of the Star Dragon

Call of the Star Dragon

Shadow of the Star Dragon

Trial of the Star Dragon

Other Science Fiction Stories

Myrmidons

Moonshot

Menelaus

Earthquake Gun

Moscow Gold

Fairchild

White Crane

The Collective Universe
The Shipwrecked Mermaid
Imposters

HE KNEW it was a calculated risk, but that wasn't going to stop Valentinian from trying his luck. At this point, the choices were all just possibilities he might have to deal with. Most of the time, the expected payoff wasn't much better than breaking even, but this particular gamble was possibly enough to alter all equations.

Not enough to get him home. At least not any time soon. The bounty on his head assured that. But if he struck it absolutely stinking rich, he could at least send some money back to his parents.

Or invite them to throw away their old lives and sail across known space and beyond to meet him in a mansion somewhere.

Valentinian didn't think Father would go for it, but he also had no idea how badly ostracized his family may have been when their only child turned out to be in league with the man who killed the Dominator. Hopefully, they weren't in prison.

Kyriaki had said that no part of the investigation she had been aware of had shown any evidence against the couple, but she had also been on the run from the law almost as long as he had.

Who knew what might have happened since then?

So he studied the planetfall on Kryuome coming up to meet him, and thought morbid thoughts. There wasn't even ground control of some sort to talk to down there, since Kryuome had nothing resembling a planetary government. Hell, most towns didn't exercise jurisdiction any farther than medium-range artillery could drop explosives on muties or raiders coming out of the desert. A whole planet down there, seventy percent land, with a population less than one hundred million souls.

"Leader, this is *Outermost*," the call came over the line. "All scans currently negative."

Good to know Glaxu was on the ball. His slayership had better sensors than *Longshot Hypothesis* did, by about an order of magnitude. If he couldn't see anybody above or below them, coming to sniff at the strangers, then there probably weren't any.

He had time, Valentinian kept telling himself. The Widow would still need to break in a new crew and get her new warship shaken down into working order before she came after them. Assuming she even guessed correctly about where to look.

"Acknowledged," Dave said from the co-pilot seat.

Valentinian was flying today, with Dave keeping watch on all the other systems. The big guy could handle something like today's mundane tasks, and he'd even landed on Kryuome by himself once.

But there was always a risk of ugly surprises, and Valentinian was too much of a control freak, at least flying, to let someone else hold his fate in their hands.

At least, not today.

A hand landed on his shoulder. Lavender, so Bayjy. No words, just silently offering strength.

He glanced back and Kyriaki had turned sideways in the doorway enough that Bayjy's long arms could reach past her. Kinda made it crowded in here, but he didn't mind. With Glaxu over in the other ship, trailing them down from orbit, this really was his entire family now. The ones he would flee across the galaxy with, if he had to.

The ones he would fight to protect.

Valentinian smiled at the two women and drew a deep breath. Big risks. Big stakes. Big payoff, if the book they had translated was accurate.

And nobody had cleared out the place before now. Treasure vaults beneath an Urlan hunting palace? What might they find, two thousand years later?

In a few hours, they would be on the ground near enough to Meeredge to hide the ship and scout the town in the truck.

And then the fun would begin, because the last time he had been through there, a few hotheads had wanted to go beyond just wiping out the local pirates and kill all humans.

They might not see Valentinian and his crew as their original saviors, so he was prepared to kill the rest if he had to.

Violence wasn't always the best solution, but it would always work, if you were prepared to unleash hell.

Valentinian was done fooling around.

[2]

DAVE

THIS WAS NOT the retirement he had originally planned when he faked his own assassination, but Dave didn't mind that much. Vee and the girls had turned out to be better family than he had ever known in the Dominion, with Valentinian and Kyriaki reminding him of his own children, Praetextatus and Euphrosyne, on good days. Everyone being about the same age just reinforced that.

Kryuome was hot today. Nasty midday weather, dry and gritty with a desert that covered most of the parts above the poisoned oceans. Records showed that it had been a lovely, green gem of a world two millennia ago, before some exceptionally angry folks hit it with a large enough asteroid to permanently alter the climate and orbital path. After dropping nuclear bombs everywhere.

Hadn't killed the planet, just most of the population. But that never stopped folks from moving in when they could get land free from the taxman. Especially if they were willing to get ugly and violent on any folks deciding they should be in charge instead later.

Nobody would conquer the population around here. Annihilate them, maybe, and bring in colonists, but nobody would really want to live here when there were so many nicer planets around to pick from.

Valentinian was driving the repulsor truck today. His prerogative, and nobody else could say they were even as good, so moot point. Glaxu was riding beside Vee in the passenger seat, scanning forward with all the sensors built into his goggles. Kyriaki was standing in the turret behind them, facing forward with her faceshield down and the twin pulse cannon hot and ready to engage anyone stupid enough to try to ambush them.

Truqtok and his folks had discovered what a suicidally-stupid idea that had been, last time. Those human thugs that were still alive the next day hadn't stuck around long when the native Jynarri in town wanted to vote on exterminating them, too.

He and Bayjy were covering the sides and rear. Vee was driving fast enough that nobody was likely to overtake them on the ground, so his eyes were watching for dots that turned into hawks approaching. No bird on this planet was larger than a hawk, and no hawk ever flew this fast, so he'd line them up with his rifle and consider shooting them down.

Holding a weapon a meter and a half long, firing caseless, rocket-powered ammunition, gave Dave a reasonable chance against even things like Glaxu's slayership, as a slug the size of his thumb would be impacting at something around ten times the speed of sound when it slammed into your aircraft or ship.

Good way to corkscrew into the ground before you knew what hit you.

But the mid-day skies of Kryuome remained empty. Probably for the best. Someone would accuse him of showing off.

Maybe.

The sled began to slow as they got to the outskirts of Meeredge. Hottest, nastiest part of the day. Bayjy would be in heaven as the heat was near to forty-eight degrees. Dave had a pair of canteens filled with water and his overrobes, same as everybody but Glaxu.

The town was quiet. Even the Jynarri went indoors in this weather and napped until the afternoon heat died down and the second souq opened for trade.

Valentinian parked them near a building, out of the way, and everyone piled out of the vehicle. Bayjy held her plasma rifle like she was hoping to bounce someone off a wall with it. Dave had his longrifle to go with everything else. Glaxu had worn his shock bracers over the dewclaws. Kyriaki had an assault pulsar with the safety off.

Vee led.

The few pedestrians they saw usually did a double-take and scampered for perceived safety as quickly as they could.

What the hell had happened in the last six months since they'd been here?

Dead silence, but that was as much a factor of the emptiness as the mood.

Valentinian headed towards the bookseller he had dealt with in the past, Marduk. As usual, Dave stationed himself outside the door, facing out on one side. Glaxu took the other, and Kyriaki followed Vee and Bayjy into the darkness.

[3]

BAYJY

SHE LOVED THE HEAT. Put a smile on her face. But Bayjy recognized a bad scene when she walked into one.

Locals were bordering on unfriendly. Near rude. Nobody waved, or catcalled, like they had before. No weapons, but anyone pointing something at this group today already had it coming, so she'd blame them.

Captain took them to the arcade. Kyrie followed the two of them into the shop like a bodyguard, which said a great deal about how that chick was reading things.

Marduk said something to her as they entered.

Took her a moment to translate it. Bastard was speaking in Urlan. Probably weren't five people on this planet that spoke it, and two of them were in here.

Oh, shit.

"What in the hell is going on, Marduk?" she

decided to play along and answer him in the same tongue.

"You and your friends are always welcome in my shop and my home," he stood and bowed a little. "But it might not be wise for you to remain in town any longer than necessary."

"What happened after we left?" Bayjy asked.

She turned to Captain and shrugged.

"I'll explain it all later, away from here," she said.

Valentinian nodded, turning towards the front of the shop and drawing his heavy flamer pistol, holding it down low to his side and keeping watch.

Bayjy still hadn't quite gotten used to the rest of the team doing that. Putting her in charge and letting her handle things. Butler would have never stood for it.

Just one of the reasons that stupid shit was dead now.

She turned back to Marduk.

"The vote was close enough," the bookseller shrugged. "The town elders decided to finish off Truqtok's people. Were in the process when the widow of Dave Hall showed up with her own, human killers. Most of my cousin Basuk's people survived, as did he, but there were hurt feelings all around. And then the widow left."

"People hold us accountable?" Bayjy asked.

"Not directly, but there are exactly four humans and one Mondi in the city of Meeredge right now," Marduk shook his head sadly. "Bad for business. Soulrake was city that took most of them in, and their money. Meeredge might fail without them. But the hotheads were loud enough and everyone was angry enough."

"Well, crap," Bayjy groused. "We came here to buy more supplies because you folks had been the nicest to us, but I don't think we'll be able to trust anything we buy now."

"No, I am sorry," Marduk nodded.

He paused for a moment and she watched a change come over the man. Jynarri. Whatever.

"No, this will not do," he suddenly announced.

She watched the man shuffle around the counter and gesture for her to back out of the cramped space so he could emerge into the noonday sun.

"If we let them win, we will never get our town back," he said, suddenly speaking spacer so everyone could understand.

He held out an elbow like a gentleman and Bayjy took it, understanding that he was offering her, and the rest of the crew, his protection.

The gang followed.

A small mob had appeared around the truck, carefully not touching it yet, in the few minutes they were gone. Maybe a dozen folk. Nobody was pointing guns at friendlies, or Kyrie probably would have just opened fire. For an ex-cop, that chick was deadly fast and kinda mean.

"This is not right," Marduk called to the group. "Not all humans are evil, regardless of what you tell each other."

"We have our city back," one of them called, stepping maybe one pace out of the group.

"Would you sacrifice all trade with outsiders?" Marduk catcalled the speaker. "Where will you get guns? Or beer? Or even food? There are not enough Jynarri to keep this town alive. Plus, these were the ones who broke Truqtok. They can be our friends. Or did you think that you and your pitiful cousins were tougher?"

The man was still close enough to the rest that he had backup, if he started something.

Bayjy could have told them what a stupid idea that was. She probably could get them all with her plasma rifle by herself, this close. The other four might not leave recognizable body parts if they got involved. Captain was already on edge. Kyrie just smelled angry.

And Big Guy…

The grumbling locals over there got a little animated, but Bayjy didn't follow their tongue well enough to read more than emotion.

Big Guy was apparently done with their shit.

Bayjy had heard stories from Kyrie and Captain both. Hadn't really believed them, because they sounded like the man was some sort of supersoldier, bad-ass warrior monk.

And then Dave handed Glaxu the rifle and snapped his baton out so hard and fast that all three pipes locked in with a single sound.

Looked like a training sword, blunt all the way around, rather than with a killing edge, like all the vids showed.

Dave walked past Marduk and right up to the mouthy punk, holding that sword down against his thigh like Captain had his pistol. Not a threat, but immediately accessible if someone needed killing.

From the way Big Guy's head moved, he was staring down at each and every one of them, making eye contact and moving on, until he got to the punk.

Bayjy couldn't remember ever being cold on this planet before now.

"Trade, or dance?" Dave announced in a mocking voice unlike anything she had ever heard from him before.

Worse, Captain and Kyrie had pivoted to cover the rear flanks, assuming she and Glaxu had Dave covered.

The locals gulped.

Something found its way to illuminating these fools before hell opened up and sucked them down into the earth. A dozen of them against Big Guy, and he was silently laughing at them, planning to kill them all with a blunt club. When they had guns.

That dude could be frightening. Death was probably jealous of the look on his face right now.

Punk backed down. Anybody without an active deathwish would right now.

Marduk was feeling feisty though.

"You," he walked right up to the dude trying to slink away and grabbing his robe. "You ask yourself where your food comes from when you get home. Where the cotton on your body originates. Think about my city before you decide to destroy it. There are more humans than Jynarri on this planet. You think they would miss us?"

Bayjy was amazed when the old guy shook the punk kid and then shoved him into the mob, but that group was happy to bug out and scampered off like roaches.

Big Guy watched them go with a sigh that almost sounded wistful, which really told Bayjy all she needed to know. She watched him kneel on one knee and *SLAM* that baton into the ground hard enough to shatter the brick he had been aiming at, but the not-sword baton collapsed into a conductor's baton.

That blow might have dented the side of the ship.

"Basuk will serve us," Marduk announced angrily. "Or he will answer to me."

Captain drove. Crowds kinda spilled out of doorways to watch, but nobody did anything.

Bayjy wondered if the punks had been terrorizing everyone else as badly as Truqtok's folks had earlier. She didn't want to be the sheriff of this place, but she could see them needing one after this.

Across town to the gated compound where the gun dealer lived. Folks here were just a little twitchy, but the news hadn't arrived yet. Captain parked under a gun tower and waved to the man with the rifle as he got out, all friendly-like.

Inside the gate, more folks were spilling out of the main building and into the inner quad. Marduk led the crew like the angry herald of a hungry god, knifing right through the assembling gunmen with shoulders and elbows until he got to the porch.

Bayjy remembered Basuk. Damn near identical cousins with Marduk, seeing them side by side, except the arms merchant was surprised and the bookdealer looked lethal.

"I have had enough," Marduk announced in a too-loud voice. "Captain Tarasicodissa and his crew were nearly attacked by one of the groups of fools. There would have been bloodshed, and all of it would have been Jynarri."

He turned and pointed at Big Guy with a snarling smile on his face.

"That human would have killed a dozen of those puppies without even breathing hard," the bookseller explained to the rest of the folks who thought they were tough. "Meeredge cannot survive like this, Basuk. You need to take charge of the city and crack faces together until people start to behave and we can have trade with the outsiders again. Otherwise, I will go broke and move to Soulrake, or some other stupid place."

Waves of grumbles passed through the group as she watched. Somehow, she had ended up on point again, like when they went into Truqtok's palace, except she really liked these people.

Be a damned shame if they had to kill everyone in the compound right now.

"What would you have me do?" Basuk asked in a calm voice.

Nobody had probably ever seen the bookseller angry, at least not from the surprised faces around her.

"Meeredge has no government but the gun," Marduk snapped. "The Jynarri will listen to you, if you decide to create something and give it force. The humans and others will come back if they thought the town was safe for their kind. That will bring the trade we need to survive. But there must be laws."

Basuk studied his cousin for several seconds as the mob of gunmen around them milled about unsteadily. Wasn't going to be a gunfight after all, from the looks of things. Marduk had just brought them along to get his cousin's attention.

Nobody likes being confronted by an angry chipmunk.

"Very well," Basuk pitched his voice loud enough to get over the grumbling and whispers. "I will appoint you governor of this city and give you a dozen men on loan for now to establish law and order. The Merchant's Guild will squeal at the taxes, but they would do that anyway."

"Me?" Marduk squealed, too.

"Who else would you suggest?" the arms merchant asked as Bayjy chuckled. "None of the others demanded that something be done to end the terrors. Only you decided to stomp into my compound and say something. Only you care enough about the city and the foreigners to do something. We will hold elections or something next year, but as you said, the city might not survive without the merchants."

Basuk turned to Bayjy and bowed, extending it to the rest of the team as her jaw fell open.

"Jenash, pick ten men and send them with my cousin," Basuk called to someone. "The stupidity is over and it is time for them to act like responsible adults again."

"There is another issue," Marduk managed to gasp out, still a little shocked at the turn of events. "My friends came to us for provisions, but I cannot trust my fellows right now. Poison. Bombs. Something."

Basuk stepped down off the porch and approached now, walking right up to the crew like Marduk had done with the gunmen. Jynarri were about human height, but skinnier, so she and Captain both looked down on the dude, to say nothing of Big Guy.

He studied Dave for a few seconds and nodded before turning to Valentinian.

"Twice you have come into my city, Captain," the man said in a relaxed voice. "Both times have changed the nature of perhaps the entire planet, and done so for the better. I wish you luck on your treasure hunt."

He turned and picked someone out of the crowd.

"Mowmash, fill six trunks with food for our friends immediately," he ordered. "Everyone else prepare to help load it, or go back to what you were doing. Marduk, the merchant's guild can reimburse me later. I'll tack it onto the bill of lading for the troopers."

Bayjy remembered to shut her mouth before her tongue got sunburnt. She was used to the crew having to use violence to protect themselves. Certainly they had done enough of it last time they were here.

But it was kinda awesome to be the good guys for once.

Of course, they still had to go into the desert for treasure. But what would a third trip to Meeredge be like?

[4]

ATHANASIA

EVEN THE NEW CREW, including the non-human members, had taken to calling her *The Widow*, but Athanasia didn't mind that much. When spoken, it tended to come out in a fearful, strangled whisper, showing just how much terror that even the newcomers had absorbed.

Dominion-427 was gone now. Returned home and taking about half of its original crew with it. The replacement captain had even recruited a few Wildspace humans, the kind that might actually be welcome in the Dominion, to fill out stations with experienced spacers.

Athanasia hadn't gotten the cream of the crop, but she had also been able to reject a few volunteers based on Captain Palaiologos's expertise. *Phoenix* was probably one of the most dangerous warships in this entire region of space as a result. She could build her own empire out here, far beyond the reach of the Dominion and be happy.

Except she could not.

Not while the man who now called himself Dave Hall was loose. Or the rest of them: Tarasicodissa or Apokapes. Athanasia added the Mondi pilot Redtip to that list for now.

Oh, she had seen the video footage. Watched that moron Butler Vidy-Wooders pick a fight with a creature a tenth his size, and ten times his brains and lethality.

That Redtip had fled immediately afterwards didn't guarantee that he was working with Tarasicodissa or Hall, but that would be her working assumption until she found the birdman again and could judge his circumstances at that moment.

The birdman may have simply decided that the humans were too stupid to work with after all, wrongly assuming that she had sent Vidy-Wooders. That would be like sending a puppy after a tiger.

She stopped herself short of working back up to a head of anger and checked her face in the mirror of her personal suite.

Blond hair starting to turn white underneath, although it would be hard to tell for years, until one day the yellow simply faded. Shoulders, hips, and waist of a Dominion warrior, even though she had been a *hausfrau* and bureaucrat for nearly thirty years. She was still up at dawn every morning doing katas and training. Only death would end that.

She never wore makeup. In the Dominion Household, all semi-public events were met with a half-mask covering nose, eyes, and forehead and decorated in a variety of styles reminiscent of animals, legends, or the Dominator's warrior regiments.

The eyes were still as blue as the late morning.

Crow's feet that hadn't been there a year ago when she started this mad quest for vengeance. Lines had been chiseled into her cheeks and lips, possibly from snarling too much.

She made a note to relax more, trying to find the comfort that she might finally own her own destiny for the first time in decades.

Hands still strong as she clenched fists. Able to kill on their own, or with a sword. At least against most men. Dave Hall was too dangerous to fight. The Dominator had still been in the top one hundred of his Caelon brigade troopers, even after the man turned fifty and was competing with men and women literally his children's age.

Athanasia drew a breath. So much to do. So little time, truly, in which to accomplish it.

That wouldn't stop her.

She opened the hatch and emerged into the salon. Stephaneria was there, face down at a desk she had added when decorating the new vessel, studying paperwork.

Athanasia drew closer silently but Stephaneria still detected her. Perhaps her sense of smell was that developed. Or she was that focused on Athanasia. They had been lovers for nearly a year now.

"Luck?" Athanasia asked carefully, aware that her normal brusqueness would be inappropriate now.

Stephaneria nodded and gestured for her to sit in the other chair.

The room was large by warship standards. Four meter ceilings, rather than the normal 2.5 or 2.9m as Dominion ships used, but it had originally been built for a M'Rai crew, and they tended towards three meters tall. Three couches framed a sitting space, along with two chairs, end tables, and a large coffee table in the middle. With the tan carpet on the floor and walls painted a soft blue with green elements like vines, you would be hard pressed to realize you weren't in a fairy tale palace somewhere.

Athanasia sat and studied her…lover? Protégé? *Successor?*

It was hard to place the woman.

A decade younger, long and whippet thin. Brown hair already streaking gray in a manner the former librarian had aggressively ignored. Stephaneria lacked the lethality of Athanasia, but made up for it with a cold, driven passion for revenge on Captain Valentinian Tarasicodissa.

For flirting with her and giving her hope, only to run off with a much younger woman. Women, actually. Two of them, ten and nearly twenty years younger than Stephaneria.

Athanasia may have played that element up when seducing the woman. Not that Stephaneria's anger had needed much to anchor itself onto.

It was amazing what passions a forty-five year old woman, divorced and childless, might have burning under a cold, calculating façade.

But then, the men and women of Bohrne Station had apparently never developed a librarian fetish.

Pity. Only Athanasia had been the one to discover the woman hidden within.

She smiled at the memory of Stephaneria's touch.

"Without the M'Rai, our options are either limited, or limitless," the librarian voice came to the fore and grounded Athanasia in vengeance, rather than seduction. "We can return to Kryuome and look for traces of *Longshot Hypothesis* and its mission.

Alternatively, we can forget them for now and you can go conquer someone."

"*We* can, Stephaneria," Athanasia corrected her. "Have you been able to discover anything?"

"Captain Palaiologos gave me access to all the logs," Stephaneria replied grimly, brushing long brown hair up out of her eyes absently. "I programmed a pattern-matching routine and let it run for six days. After that, I have been slowly filtering out false positives by hand."

Athanasia could detect the excitement vibrating quietly under the surface of the woman's words, like an impending orgasm. Silent and still for the longest time before coming to the surface in one long, volcanic eruption.

"You found him?" Athanasia felt her breath grow short, her heart start to pound.

"Maybe," the librarian's mouth said, but her eyes told the truth.

Athanasia kissed the mouth to prevent more lies. Stephaneria wrapped arms about her and they were suddenly standing, pressed against each other in their excitement that they might both have vengeance on the two men that had wronged them.

And the women who had helped.

THE MAP WAS UGLY, no two ways about it. Iulianus understood that he was merely the Chief Operating Officer of this vessel, rather than the executive, but he did at least have a level of professional expertise the two women lacked.

Stephaneria Meers-Bolat was far better at research and data manipulation than he was. And she was probably smarter than him on a purely intellectual basis. Athanasia had spent a generation as the wife of the most important, and lethal, man in the entire Dominion, and had run his Household. Two extremely capable and deadly players that he did respect as partners.

But this was warfare, and Iulianus Palaiologos was a captain in the Dominion Armada, the most feared naval force in several sectors.

At least he had been. Like many others, he had allowed the woman to seduce him away from his duty. Or perhaps deeper into it.

His orders had been to keep Athanasia from ever

returning to the Dominion. There was no leeway there, unless he was returning with just her head stored for travel. If he remained with her, that gave him greater opportunity to keep her at a safe distance, as his own career was over until she was dead and he could be free.

The perks were good, though. Command of a warship roughly equivalent to a Dominion Poniard, the escorts for the ZoneStrikers and larger vessels. Tiny, perhaps, by his old standards, but most certainly more capable than almost any other vessel they would encounter in Wildspace.

He studied the two women across the table and considered the other perks as well. Athanasia had been willing to share herself in every sense of the word, to bind him to her mission. Stephaneria had proven to be a willing accomplice.

If he was the junior partner in this venture, there were worse places to be.

Like the map spread out between them.

Dominion-427, his old command, had been an Assault Courier, an armed transport designed to deliver VIPs to destinations in comfort and security. It had been equipped with advanced sensors compared to *Phoenix*, but the M'Rai had only ever been interested in plunder and pillage.

They had spent several days in orbit of Kryuome on their first trip, scanning all of the surface in spite of the general expectation of the locals that Tarasicodissa was near the south pole looking for a hidden, Urlan base. Like that would have been missed by the men and women who did…this.

The map was huge and showed the brutal efficiency that someone had brought to warfare. Two meters by six, pieced together out of the plotter and blown up. There was a map layer showing background radiation that had been caused by nuclear weapons. Some of the places shown would be lethal in a matter of weeks. Others were merely hazards that could be tolerated for months or perhaps as much as a year, depending on your medical team and metabolism.

It was actually two pictures, side by side.

Before and after, as it were.

The first had been taken almost as soon as *Dominion-427* hit orbit, before they realized that there was nobody below handling landing coordination. The Librarian had marked a fuzzy image that looked like a capital-T, once the computers had washed out wind and heat distortions.

In the second picture, the same image was gone, like it had never existed. Overnight, based on the timeslots printed at the bottom.

Iulianus returned to the first image and studied it closer. The seraphs on the letter gave it away. It was actually more of a Y shape, but very flat across the bar, with a pair of oversized engines at the ends of the spars.

An Anuradhan cargo transport. One located an extremely vast distance from home.

There was always the chance that it was not the vessel *Longshot Hypothesis*, but Iulianus wasn't willing to lose money on that bet.

"As good a working theory as any," Iulianus finally said, fixing his gaze on Stephaneria and smiling. "Amazing quality of research, as well."

She smiled back at him.

Had no man ever appreciated this woman for her

mind? Fools. If the body lacked the fleshiness that the Dominion and other cultures venerated, there was no doubt she was capable of really thinking. And other passions.

"However," he continued abruptly, "unlike *Dominion-427*, *Phoenix* is incapable of landing on the surface of any planet. We would need to travel down in one of the cargo balingers. Those are large and sturdy, but incapable of engaging the Mondi vessel if it is about. The weapons on *Phoenix* will be incapable of protecting us while we are away."

"Stealth and guile, Captain," Athanasia spoke for the first time in several minutes.

She reached out a long, slender hand and touched a spot on the map clear up at the northwest corner. Iulianus noted a village or fortress of some sort. Small and distant, perhaps forty kilometers away from where the ship had parked, but close enough that they might see an overflight and respond.

"The T'Brask," she said. "The so-called mutants of the Juxx Wastelands. *Longshot Hypothesis* would have been invisible, if they were careful, but note the roads entering into the ruins, and how they largely follow the safest bands of lower radiation. It would appear that the locals can detect such things, but still travel to the remains of the city often enough, so perhaps they understand whatever value brought Tarasicodissa."

He paused and did the math in his head, unused to thinking like a pirate admiral after a career of making sure the tea was served at just the right temperature and steeping.

"The balinger will hold up to sixteen, with supplies for a week on the ground," he thought out loud. "Water will be the keenest resource, as I would not trust anything on the surface anyway, until it had been thoroughly purified. Perhaps a dozen would be a safer force, to reduce consumption and increase supplies. We also do not have effective ground transport if we leave the shuttle any distance away, short of purchasing one or two from local merchants, as Tarasicodissa apparently did last time he was here. Do we wish the natives to know our presence?"

"No," Athanasia said immediately. "We cannot know what relationship they may have established with our quarry, so we cannot risk them giving warning. Plan for a dozen, including myself and Stephaneria. We will determine where the ship has landed and find a safe spot close enough we can approach under darkness."

"Standard Dominion procedures include me remaining with the vessel in orbit, madam," he stated carefully.

Technically, he could just abandon her there. Perhaps issue secret orders to one of the crew to kill the woman down on the surface, but what would that get him?

The ability to return home to a gray existence for another decade or so until he retired? A quiet medal before being forgotten or cast aside?

Iulianus Palaiologos had no illusions that he would be welcomed home any more warmly than the Widow. Even if he delivered his old masters her head.

Not every mid-life crisis involved taking up piracy, but he had found passions that had been hidden behind masks for so long that he had forgotten ever feeling them.

Athanasia was studying him, like she could read the words in thought bubbles over his head.

She might, considering her past. But she had also given him reasons to remain. To even enjoy dereliction of duty bordering on mutiny.

The Widow smiled at him now. Stephaneria did the same.

"We have two of the cargo vessels, Iulianus," she said with a knowing smile. "If I get into trouble on the surface, I will expect you to come riding to my rescue with a team of killers."

Truly, the cherry on top, to appeal to the knight-in-shining-armor fantasy that drove most people into the Dominion Armada.

Fire-breathing berserkers joined the Solar Guard and tried to earn a spot in one of the Assault Brigades.

He would serve by waiting. But he would be rewarded for his duty.

[6]
VALENTINIAN

THE BASIN HADN'T CHANGED in the months they had been gone, at least as far as Valentinian could tell. And probably not in the last century either.

Descending from altitude, both ships had scanned the city, the mutie camp, and anything else that might have been even remotely interesting or out of place. All the sensors Bayjy had built were still there, but none of them were transmitting, so Valentinian couldn't tell if the locals had found them, or they had just failed. Short of walking into the village and asking, there wasn't any way to be sure.

But they had taken their time approaching, remaining out of sight up there while *Outermost* scanned things. Nobody was living in the ruins that he could tell, and even the T'Brask would start dying if they spent all their time down there for long.

In the end, there had been nothing to do but chance it. *Longshot Hypothesis* and *Outermost* had both landed just beyond the southern tip of the fourteen-mountain-range that hooked westward like a crescent to catch winds. In the old days, they had also funneled rain, keeping the area lush enough that a huge lake had once existed there, with that Urlan hunting lodge not far from the shores.

Before. When the planet was still green.

Valentinian shaded his eyes as he checked the western skies, but there was no hint of weather. Near as he could guess, the place might have a rainy season that lasted a week or three, but mostly just wind that picked up sand and chucked it at you like bullets. Occasionally, probably monstrous windstorms that blackened the sky, but even those were rare enough that the city was blown clear after a week or a month.

Otherwise, everything would have disappeared under the sands by now.

"You're contemplative this morning," Dave offered as he wandered out of the rear bay of the ship.

Kyriaki was on top of the vessel with a long rifle, watching for trouble coming. If she stood up, she probably looked like a sand nymph emerging from the desert, given the netting they had strung across both ships after landing.

"Got a bad feeling about this one, Dave," Valentinian shrugged to himself and turned to his giant first mate.

"Anything in particular?" the man asked.

"No, or I would have done something else," Valentinian shook himself and headed back towards where the truck was parked.

He had only stepped outside as an excuse to breathe overhot air and try to leave all his misgivings here, instead of carrying them forward. Wasn't working, but he didn't want to tell everyone that. They had enough to worry about.

"We're packed," Dave announced as he followed. "As much water as we can comfortably carry now, with both ships set to tap as much out of the air as the vaporators can pull. Plus we've got the portable unit."

"Six days, give or take?" Valentinian asked as he climbed into the truck and did a quick preflight.

Bayjy waved from where she was doing an inventory. The bed of the truck was packed so full Valentinian was surprised that the five of them would be able to get aboard, but Bayjy and Dave had both assured him it would work.

"Give or take, yeah," Dave agreed. "We'll want to swing back in about four and refill these tanks, just so we aren't pushing our margins, but we can leave the rest of the camp over there, so maybe just you and Bayjy will need to handle that part."

Valentinian nodded. They had gamed all this out on the flight to Chatosig, and then again on the way here. Now all they had to worry about was the Widow maybe showing up with combat troops and finding or destroying the ship, so he'd gone ahead and disabled a number of systems by removing certain power couplers and burying them nearby.

If they had to leave in a hurry, *Longshot* would be in trouble, but *Outermost* would be able to lift quickly, and anybody wanting to argue right-of-way with Glaxu was in for a rude surprise, so Valentinian didn't worry too much.

He also had a team of killers on his side, so anything less than a full mob of muties wasn't that serious a threat.

"Clear?" he yelled as the repulsors powered up with a hum.

"Clear," Bayjy called back.

Valentinian looked all directions, but Glaxu was outside running laps in the heat and Dave had stepped back, so he backed the truck into the sunlight. The afternoon sun was brutal, but he wanted to be able to do at least the first part of this mission with sunlight. He had purchased goggles that would help him drive at night with the headlights off, but you still had to move slowly.

Still better than flashing bright lights all over the basin for some distant watcher to maybe notice and come investigate.

Nothing would blow up this mission faster than running into the muties. Even the Widow probably wasn't as bad.

At least that was what he told himself.

The sound of the truck had apparently been a dinner bell or something. Glaxu came in off the desert sand like the hunting bird predator he was. Bayjy and Dave walked out of the bay.

Valentinian looked up and realized that Kyriaki was descending on the outside of the ship instead of coming through the interior locks, so he just kind of sat and stared at her bottom as she came down the ladder.

They still hadn't even kissed. Something about the confines of the ship, and the tension of everything else as they tried to outthink Dave's wife and her mad quest for vengeance, or whatever it had turned into now that the woman had a warship capable of doing damned near anything she wanted in Wildspace.

Kyriaki had a nice bottom. But seriously, that would just be one more thing on the list of changes right now. Valentinian didn't have the energy for one more.

And she seemed to feel the same way. They would acknowledge it with a look and a chuckle as they found themselves alone in the armory, or moving boxes. Jokes about screenwriters just made it funnier.

"Bayjy, seal us up," Valentinian finally came back to the present tense with a wistful sigh he kept inside.

"You got it," the woman laughed.

Valentinian looked and realized the ship was already secured and everyone was in the process of finding seats.

Whoops.

Maybe when they got to someplace really civilized, moreso than Chatosig-Six. Or perhaps down on the surface where he and Kyriaki could take a weekend and get a hotel room with good food delivery options.

After Kryuome, they would all either be rich, or needing something to distract themselves from the terrible letdown of discovering the place had been looted a thousand years ago and it had all been a wild goose chase, regardless of the stories he could tell in bars for the rest of his life.

Something to look forward to as he studied the sky and wondered who he would see dropping out of it like a giant hawk.

[7]
KYRIAKI

WITH HER HAIR up under a helmet and the faceshield down and locked in, Kyriaki felt like she was in another world. One defined by the targeting reticle located at the end of the twin barrels that sniffed the desert sands like an angry dragon.

Nothing electronic was going to last for long around here, so she had settled for better electronic optics in her goggles and left it at that. The engines weren't so loud that she couldn't hear someone talking in a normal voice.

They would only have to yell if she was using the twin pulsar, and at that point other people would probably be shooting as well.

The afternoon sun was on her left as they crossed sands, rock, and scrub where plants had found enough water to survive. The T'Brask village was perhaps eighty kilometers north and a little west as they came around the southern-most of the mountains in the Crescent.

Nothing moved that she could see as they

traversed the Juxx Wastes, and Kyriaki preferred it that way.

The others saw her as a stone killer, she knew that. But she had been a cop, once upon a time. Arrest bad guys and bring them to justice, rather than indiscriminately hose down a building with heavy beam fire. That had come later.

Kyriaki was a pirate now. No two ways about it. She could never go back to the Dominion and put on the white beret and maroon bodysuit of the Security Bureau. And there were no comparable governments in Wildspace that needed a cop like her, unless she wanted to do something like the Sheriff of Bohrne Station had done. Meeredge would need such a constable, one of these days, but she didn't see herself there either.

Kyriaki studied the back of Valentinian's head as he drove. Wondered how much longer it would be before he settled enough into a new routine that she could consider breaking it and not driving him sideways in the process.

Without the crew of *Longshot Hypothesis* keeping her sane and grounded, Kyriaki wasn't sure what she would do, so she wasn't going anywhere, but she also knew Vee wouldn't step out of the emotional shell he carried around until he was ready.

At the same time, she appreciated that he treated her with adult honesty, brutal as it might be at times. He had never lied to her since she came aboard the ship as a stowaway with a detonator, wondering if she was going to assassinate the man or surrender her soul to him.

Treated her like a friend, rather than a tumble. Had been, as far as she knew, entirely celibate, save for that one night at Bohrne Station when he could have had his pick of three women instead.

Kyriaki smiled to herself, under the mask. Given that the librarian had apparently joined forces with the Widow, from Glaxu's description, he might still have that option soon. Bayjy was afraid she might break the man in the throes of an orgasm. The librarian probably just wanted to kill him.

Only Kyriaki was sure she'd leave him alive afterwards. She was after his mind. And maybe his soul.

But she was a hunter. She could outwait him. And the others.

A line on the horizon drew her attention.

"First waypoint marker," she called loud enough to the rest of them. They were sitting down, hunkered against the heat and biting sand, so she had the best view. "Bear right about ten degrees."

Valentinian raised one hand in brief acknowledgement and then she felt the truck shift, biting on the one corner and slewing around just enough that she let herself lean into the ring that upheld the turret.

Three minutes and they were there.

Valentinian, perhaps showing where his head was, pulled the truck behind a small rock outcropping and parked. It wasn't much. Hell, he could probably see over it just fine sitting down, but the man was as much under cover as he could get.

And she'd been around him enough now to understand that he was always like that.

The silence as he landed on the skids and cut the repulsors entirely was like night falling. Just the light breeze mostly out of the south, the sun's brutal heat, and the spicy smell of the desert itself.

Kyriaki decided she needed a break to walk around, so she climbed down out of the ring and over the various boxes until she was on sand. She wore desert boots, and even through the heavy soles she could feel the heat as she moved.

This was Bayjy's operation now, so she, Dave, and Glaxu fanned out enough to keep watch, but followed the woman. Valentinian stayed leaned against the solid steel plate that kept the wind off his knees and stomach as he drove. She considered joining him, but decided she wanted to see Bayjy's latest masterwork instead.

Before, they had set up paired optical sensors on the northern approaches. Something moving would break the beam and trigger an alarm and a camera.

That was when they had discovered just how many animals came out at night to hunt and feed. And were just tall enough to break the light.

So Bayjy had gone back to the drawing board.

The so-called road they had just joined was more of a track that had been hammered down by generations of wheeled vehicles traversing it. Maybe centuries.

The T'Brask didn't appear to have any flyers using repulsortech, just a couple of what looked like airplanes with propellers to push them through the sky. Those might sneak up on this crew, but they couldn't hover, and they had only seen the two on scans. One might not even work.

But the rest would come by ground. Four- and six-wheeled buggies not that much different from the simple frame and mesh sides of this truck. One of them, from Glaxu's images, even had a similar turret, although Basuk had not known what heavy weaponry the tribes might have.

There were a number of arms dealers on this planet making an exceptional living providing arms and equipment to the desert dwellers in trade for whatever the locals might have acquired. Every season saw more than one treasure hunter head into the deeps looking for their fortune. Kyriaki assumed that most ended up in the stewpots of the crazier tribes, and their pretty equipment bought more guns.

The boys would face such a fate, Basuk has assured her. She and Bayjy had something worse to look forward to. For Kyriaki, that meant her mind had gone to a dark, forbidding place where excessive violence was her starting point, before she got ugly.

But Bayjy was irrepressible. All that sass just got brighter when she got stressed. Still couldn't use her plasma rifle like a precision instrument, but she didn't need to, with the rest of the team around.

Instead, the woman had developed a seismograph.

"That's all it takes?" Kyriaki asked as she found herself looking into the hole Bayjy had cleared with her hands.

"That's it, babe," Bayjy grinned up at her in purple.

The thing was a black, plastic device Bayjy had printed in the machine shop in about a dozen pieces, with a bunch of wires leading to a universal chip that the lavender woman had programmed in her spare time.

"Watch," Bayjy wiped her hands with a towel as she stood.

Far be it for Bayjy to wear layers of cloth to keep the heat off like the rest of them. Today she was in light capris and a sleeveless white T-shirt with nothing under it or over it, although her so-called *Winter Expedition Gear* would come out of a bag about the time the sun went down.

Bayjy pulled her card-reader out and flipped through screens until she found the one she wanted and pressed a virtual button.

On the ground, the seismograph chirped once and a little red light activated. Bayjy pushed sand and dirt over it with her foot until the black was gone.

"Captain, all set to calibrate," Bayjy called.

Kyriaki hadn't really been paying attention to the testing portion to know what happened next. Her job was security, so she hopped up on the rock and spun slowly in place. From up here, she was even taller than Dave.

Vee powered the truck up and drove a wide circle, coming out of the desert again about a hundred meters up the road and aimed this way at a relatively high speed. The roostertail of crap in the air behind him wasn't all that big, but anything except a dust devil would draw the eye, so they had to pay attention to their horizons now.

Nothing moving but a few birds, probably hoping they dropped something edible.

Valentinian popped back off the road a ways down and circled back, this time pulling up close to Bayjy before spinning in place and coming to rest, pointed nose-first into the basin.

"Okay," Bayjy called in a voice that sounded happy. "I've got it baselined to react to eighty percent of the sled's noise. We're assuming that a truck on wheels will be harder on the ground, so even something light should cause the system to wake up and call us. I want to put a camera a mile or so further up the track and leave it fixed and hidden. That lets us react to the sensor and see who's coming."

"Two-wheeler with an engine?" Dave asked, never taking his eyes off the horizon.

"One probably gets by, unless he drives almost over the seismograph," Bayjy admitted. "But more than one should be as loud on the ground as a truck. And a herd of goats or something would also set it off if they stampeded, but I haven't seen anything like that."

"Correct," Glaxu chirped. "Such things are exceptionally rare in the Wastes, and appear to be domesticated. Wild herds can be found in both temperate latitudes, but I never developed the need to hunt them."

Kyriaki supposed that might have been an option Glaxu was reduced to while trying to find someone friendly enough and capable enough to fix his overdrive before they came along. And one goat killed and dried would probably have fed a Mondi for weeks.

"So we're golden," Bayjy said. "Or you people are and I'm the awesomest shade of mauve y'all ever been blessed to lay eyes on. We ready to get stupid, Captain?"

"More stupid, Little Miss Mauve?" Kyriaki heard Vee laugh back at the irrepressible Bayjy Endon.

"You know. Whatever."

Kyriaki laughed with the rest of them as they

loaded back into the truck and started what Bayjy had called the penetration run. Where things would get riskier by the hour, and nobody knew when bad guys would pop out from behind cover and cause problems.

Other bad guys.

[8]

GLAXU

AT A FLETCHLING, Glaxu had always been taught that the Mondi were the most dangerous species in the galaxy. As species went, that might still be true, but he had come to appreciate that the humans of the Spinward Reaches were probably as dangerous in general, and the four around him were at the higher end of whatever stick you wanted to use to measure.

Like Bayjy, Glaxu's kind had been built for weather like this. Evolution in his case, and intelligent design in hers. Either way, the heat brought him comfort. As did finally belonging to a nest again.

He knew the crew of *Longshot Hypothesis* liked and respected him, but until he had come out of warp and found the ship waiting for him where Captain had specified, there had always been a niggling feeling in the back of his head that perhaps they had lost trust in him. Or that the fear of his triple-cross of the Widow failing had overwhelmed their good sense, and they wouldn't be there.

He could get home now. Wherever that might be, but as far as he was concerned, it was sitting on the riskier wing of *Longshot Hypothesis* as they moved.

The road Captain was taking was a thin trail that would take them to the top of the third mountain from the south. They all had names, at least in the ancient records Captain and Bayjy were using to plot their salvageness, but such names were in Urlan, and Bayjy got angry when she had to speak that tongue.

As a result, everything was merely a number, counting from the southern edge where the dewclaw of mountains simply vanished back into the highlands on three sides.

Glaxu turned his head to the left and let the computer systems build up several hundred images of the northwestern approaches. Unlike Kyriaki, he had always kept the best electronics he could afford, since his helmet was with him whenever he was flying or now riding in the truck.

He keyed the button on the side of his skull and turned back to face center, confident that the others would notice any troubles arising in the next three minutes.

The computer routine was originally designed to spot ships trying to hide in the darkness, by comparing snapshots of the stars in the background and noticing movement or occultation.

Today, he zoomed in on the thick band of darkness just visible at the horizon and let the semi-intelligent machines wash out haze and compare each shot to the next. He had already imported scans from other directions, so this merely improved the quality of the three-dimensional representation that it held.

He could even count trucks visible on this side of the low stone walls that surrounded the place. Nobody had moved. That was good.

They had an escape route planned against need. This very road they were driving up had been previously mashed down by other vehicles, so someone came up here at least annually.

Granted, if they had to flee now, it would be over dangerously rough terrain, but the sorts of places that wheels could not take you with any speed, giving them time to build up a lead.

Glaxu still thought that Captain should have brought his ship into a hover close against the face of their target cliff and let not-Dave-Hall leap from the bay with ropes to keep him from falling off a mountain. As it was, they would get there not long before dusk and have to camp overnight.

"How good are your optics, Glaxu?" Bayjy's voice suddenly intruded.

He turned to her blankly and blinked through his goggles before the words finally registered.

"Exceptional," he finally said. "I have a fully-realized projection of the village now. Would you like to see it?"

"What about the ruins?" she asked.

More blankness. Was this shock? Was that allowed?

"Do we not have up-to-date scans, Bayjy?" he asked, at something of a loss.

"Those are from the ships and the past, Glaxu," she tilted her head at him in the perfect imitation of a Mondi Elder. Or his mother.

He wondered if she had picked it up from him, or if it was a sentient thing.

"You are correct," he agreed, still trying to find the thread of the conversation.

"Good, so do your thing with the ruins while we're up here so we have more angles," she smiled.

Irrepressible was the term Captain and Kyriaki used to refer to the woman. It fit.

"Stand by," he said.

Glaxu braced himself and triggered his systems to lock on the ruins below and scan. They were not on a cliff's edge here, but the slope of the mountain right now would let him scan for perhaps as much as ten seconds. He could wait and build up a larger database of images when they got to the top, and thus add a time element to the visualizations they could project.

Truly, a sneakier thing on her part. Mondi were in the present tense when fighting. Obviously a good salvager like Bayjy was concerned with the small movements over time that perhaps represented entropic decay.

How things evolved over time as bits decayed and thus made it either easier or harder to break in and rob the place. What was it she had said?

The fewest cuts in the fastest time meant the greatest profit.

Yes. Senior Cutter Bayjy Endon was just as great a warrior as Valentinian Tarasicodissa or Dave Hall or Kyriaki Apokapes.

He just needed to learn from her.

[9]

DAVE

From up here, it wasn't all that impressive looking, but Dave was also seeing the village from a distance of perhaps fifty kilometers or so and using the scope on his rifle. Simple glass, rather than something more advanced.

Or prone to failure in the harsh environment around them.

One village. Space for perhaps fifteen hundred people inside the walls, assuming the T'Brask were of a human scale. He'd never met one, and everyone was smaller than Dave Hall anyway, so it was hard to judge.

Stone walls that appeared to have been comprised in part of outcroppings linked together with rubble and then flattened on top for beings with guns to defend the place.

Dave wondered who might raid the mutants of the Juxx Wastelands enough that they needed protection. Large predators, perhaps mutated up from smaller creatures given time and radiation?

Evolutionary pressures in this environment would compress thousands of years of change into generations for those who survived.

Or perhaps it was a prison, and the walls were to keep the slaves from escaping? Where would one go, but to die in the desert itself? But maybe that was preferable to the stew pots Basuk had warned them about.

The man Dave Hall used to be could have simply ordered the village annihilated before the inhabitants decided to pose a threat to his forces. Even a thousand crazed berserkers would have lasted only hours against the Caelons.

But that was part of the joy of discovering he liked being Dave Hall. He could ignore those people and allow them to seek out their own destiny. At least until they decided to give him grief and he had to respond in kind.

Dave laughed to himself and took the rifle off the monopod he had been using to stabilize it.

"What's so funny?" Kyriaki asked from across the small area where they were seated.

Bayjy and Vee were still busy setting up a couple of cameras and making sure they had the images aligned just right. Glaxu had gone for a brief run around the encampment, mostly just to burn off excess energy.

That left him and Kyriaki to hang around waiting.

"Looking back at the man I used to be," Dave said. "Comparing him to Dave Hall and laughing at how far I've come from that dour, stonehearted bastard. How much I like being me."

"Being you?" she asked in a confused tone that reminded Dave she was his daughter's age and had lived almost as monastic a lifestyle as a Dominator did.

Old age and treachery will still overcome youth and skill, young lady.

"I've been a number of men over the years, decades, Kyriaki," Dave rested the rifle against his leg, barrel up and safety on, as he turned to face her. "It's a healthy thing to occasionally take stock of your personality and make changes. Keeps you from turning into a spiteful, vicious, shrew like my ex-wife."

"Was she always like that?" Kyriaki asked, careful in her tone.

The Dominion did not discuss these things in public. Nor anywhere except within close bonds of friendship.

Masks everyone wore to hide behind.

"She was not," Dave said with a wry grin. "Driven and lethal, yes, but the years of running my Household wore on her. I think it was the empty nest element that probably did her in. With Euphrosyne and Praetextatus both grown up and gone, I think she started to worry about when the next challenger to my power would rise."

"How long did you have?" Kyriaki pressed, shifting out of nervousness and into curiosity. "Before someone was dangerous enough to threaten you?"

"I'm fifty-two now," Dave shrugged. "In as good a shape as the kids I trained with nearly every day, and they were your age. Historically, most Dominators fall off their physical peak around forty and their leadership will carry them for another ten to twenty years. There weren't any serious threats on my horizon for maybe a decade."

"Then why'd you do it?" she asked.

Dave shrugged. He'd had this conversation with Vee, early on, but he'd left out the tidbits about who he really was when he did.

"You can't retire from that job," Dave said. "Too many top people have to die when a Dominator takes power, so it's yours until someone rises that can take it away from you. If it was up to me, I'd have changed things so a Dominator lasted twenty years and then could retire and become an elder statesman or something. But the culture fears all the palace intrigues of a former Dominator."

"So you had to fake your own death and run away?" Kyriaki cocked her head at him.

"Would have succeeded, if you weren't so damned good at your job," he smiled. "Fly with Vee for six months or a year, and then change identcards one day and vanish. Until someone broke into the forward airlock while we were in the process of fleeing Bohrne Station the first time."

"I needed to become someone else, too," Kyriaki's voice turned introspective now. He sat motionless and let her think aloud. "But I wasn't approaching it rationally. The first time I was close enough to Valentinian to smell him, something went off in my head and that pissed me off even worse than that unexpected desire did. Made me go looking for a reason to nail his ass to a wall and toss him in a cell."

"Is that why you didn't arrest me?" Dave asked. "I would have gone, because all of Vee's problems I caused."

"Wouldn't have saved him," Kyriaki sighed as

Dave listened. "My bosses would have brought him in and put him under the truth serum to see what he knew. And probably killed him anyway so they didn't have to explain the truth to outsiders. That's why I let both of you go."

"And Athanasia showed up two days later to arrest us," Dave nodded.

"Hours after you had fled," she nodded back. "At that point, I had run out of rope as well. Eventually, she would have started asking me pointed questions and I probably would have gone under the serum."

"It's a good thing I picked Vee, then, of all the captains I had reviewed."

"Why is that?" she asked. "Wouldn't others have been better cover?"

"Vee was distraction, Kyriaki," Dave smiled. "You were so busy looking at him you forgot I was there. Your bosses would have had the same problem. Ex-cadet to the Dominion Armada, thrown out of the Gymnasia Dominia under questionable circumstances. Won the money to buy this ship in what he called *another* crooked poker game. They would dig as hard as I did, and not find a damned thing. Lower middle class family. Father a retired civilian captain. Mother a homemaker. No siblings. No scandals. Nothing."

"Sorry I ruined all your plans, Dave," she said after a few moments of silence.

"It worked out for the best," he replied. "Vee has managed to save all of us so far. Our job is to pay him back by hopefully finding the pot at the end of the rainbow."

"Then what?" her voice had suddenly gone small and cold.

"Then hopefully you two find a room somewhere and figure out what you mean to each other," Dave said. "I'm too old to start another family, but not so old I want to retire anywhere just yet, so if Bayjy's utterly wealthy, I might hire on with her when she buys her own ship. Or go visit Glaxu's kind. The future starts tomorrow, Kyriaki Apokapes. You made the choices that got you here. After today, you make better ones."

She lapsed into silence, digesting the nuggets of painful experience he could polish up and call wisdom.

Hopefully she would listen. Or not. Tomorrow would take care of itself.

First, they just had to find a treasure.

[10]
STEPHANERIA

STEPHANERIA CARESSED the pistol as she drew it from
the holster, smelling the sharp tang of the lubricant
on the weapon that always made her think of limes.
The weight felt just right in her hand.

She closed her off-eye and breathed calmly out as
she connected her sight, her weapon, and infinity in a
single line.

The jump as she fired felt perfect. The target had a
hole where his heart should have been.

They shouldn't have been surprised, so
Stephaneria was almost offended as the men around
her watching. The ones suggesting that they should
teach her how to shoot. Her uncle was a sheriff, and
had been a lawman of one kind of another for as long
as she could remember. He had taught her how to kill
something, someone, if she needed to as a little girl.

Her husband hadn't really understood that side of
her, but he'd never apparently even noticed that his
wife wasn't as boringly two-dimensional as he was.
To this day, Stephaneria could not identify the point

at which she had chosen to settle for someone like him, rather than carving her own life out of the galaxy.

Maybe it had been the poverty that was never far away in Laurentia. Strauss had offered her a social and economic stability that was probably unrivaled, since he was an accountant. She could remain a homemaker and busybody, secure that he would never be out of work for long, and would never suffer greatly from any economic ups or downs.

But she had never anticipated how boring it would be. Stultifying. Monotonous. Even books had not given her enough escape, no matter how many she read. Nor research, when she had the time and energy to wander down any rabbit hole that might catch her fancy, while her husband went to work and crunched numbers day in and day out.

Until one day, Strauss cracked.

In retrospect, they were already strangers by that point. She had never had an affair solely because the men she could have found in her social circle had all been knockoff copies of Strauss, so there was nothing they could offer her. Random strangers had never registered either, as she had always compared them to the powerful, interesting men and women in her books and somehow forgotten along the way that writers have to amp things up to extraordinarily levels to keep the reader engaged.

And the world around her was so bland when she looked up.

Until Strauss announced that he was divorcing her to move in with the little bimbo currently pregnant with his child. The child she had never given him, because it had never seemed that important.

Or she had never actually been paying attention when he said something. That was a measure of their marital bliss for the full decade it has lasted.

Forty. Alone. Withered on the vine, perhaps, when Laurentia still worshiped the first bloom of adulthood and considered thirty ancient enough that others she knew in her social circles had already begun treatments and surgery to convince their husbands that they were secretly unaging vampires only eighteen years old.

Uncle Ramazan had found her a job, surrounding her with as many books as she could perhaps ever read, and whatever research projects might wander in for help.

It had been enough. Perhaps.

Until *he* walked in and flashed those pretty, blue-green eyes at her. Confident and dominant. Stoking energies Stephaneria had forgotten she possessed.

And then he ran off with a bimbo. Just another Strauss.

They were all like that, weren't they?

Ramazan always used to say that emotions did not belong anywhere near a firearm. That you should practice your marksmanship in a calm, detached state of mind. If you were emotional, you began to conflate the two, and one day you might find your response to great emotional pain involved a gun.

But that was a teenage girl. The adult had lived decades in an emotional desert, bereft of even human touch by a distant husband who had eventually sought solace in a child young enough to be his.

That was the old Stephaneria. The cold, vacuous

bitch who never felt anything but emptiness. Before she had discovered an unconquerable rage at men, and the calming, maddening touch of Athanasia.

Even Iulianus Palaiologos did not drive her to any great passions, but there were times when she discovered needs and he was confident enough in himself to service her desires before seeing to his own.

Stephaneria lowered the barrel of the pistol and imagined Strauss standing ten meters away with that stupid, love-struck puppydog look on his face as he told her about the new life he was leaving her for.

The next shot took him in the groin. The third in the face, as did the fourth. Several more destroyed his groin with the same sort of fire he probably felt these days from whatever venereal diseases his little tramp had picked up while trolling for a new sugar daddy.

Stephaneria raised her barrel back to the sky as she had been trained and set the safety. There was no sky here, deep in the bowels of *Phoenix*, the bird that symbolized rebirth in more ways than one.

She turned and fixed the rangemaster with a calm, deliberate stare that challenged his very manhood to improve on her shooting. Or top it somehow with his own.

The score itself wasn't all that great. The target had rings on the heart and the farther you were from center mass, the lower your official score. She hadn't missed any of her targets by more than a few centimeters, even at this range.

From the haunted look in the man's eyes, he knew that. Knew that she was punishing all the men in the universe for wronging her, even the ones she might later allow to worship at her feet.

Oh yes, Athanasia had taught her the proper way to approach men such as this rangemaster.

Now she just needed to find Valentinian Tarasicodissa and remind him of what he had walked away from.

VALENTINIAN

MORNING. The desert was cold enough that Valentinian woke to find dew on things as he emerged from the brown tent he shared with Dave. Glaxu was already up and had run a number of laps around the camp. Dave was making coffee. The two women would probably be up shortly.

The view from up here was magnificent. Radiation levels were actually kind of low, so they had just bombed this area with conventional munitions. Maybe strafed it in passing during an assault drop to destroy what the oldest maps showed as an observatory set back from the ridge and on the darker side of things for a better view of space.

You didn't need something like this when you could put a more powerful tool into planetary or solar orbit, but this sort of thing was as old as any civilization he had ever heard about. One of the first marks of culture was looking at the stars and trying to figure out how everything else worked.

Valentinian took a mug of coffee from an

otherwise silent Dave and just considered those ruins. T'Ilard and the imperial hunting lodge palace complex. Or whatever it was. Valentinian wasn't that much of a scholar of the Urlan, since he'd grown up in the Dominion and those folks were mostly discounted as legends that far from this part of Wildspace.

The cameras were in place. With Bayjy's genius for electronics, they had several secured channels watching various parts of the basin so they could detect anyone trying to sneak up on them, just as soon as the various zone alarms went off.

If he had more time, Valentinian would have just put a small camp up here and watched the radioactive ruins below for a month or two so he could establish the rhythms of whatever political or religious activities brought the T'Brask into the hot zones regularly enough that roadways survived. But background radiation up here was bad enough that he didn't want to risk it. And nobody had any clue how soon the Widow might decide to come looking for them here.

Or even how long it would take to open up that tomb over there, or whatever it was, and loot the place to the bare walls. Which was really all he cared about.

Valentinian really didn't appreciate becoming more introspective. Sounded too much like growing up, even if he was the youngest person here. Being in charge did that. When it was just him and Artaxerxes, they'd been hustling constantly just to stay above water.

They'd be there again soon if this didn't pan out. Every single day it cost money just to exist.

Maintenance equipment costs. Food. Hell, even oxygen and water when you were docked to a station and maybe offloading sludge from the waste tanks.

Adding a hydroponics bay back in would actually help a lot, since that would generate fresh food and fish regularly, while consuming fertilizer.

But he still had to hustle. And that required money.

Valentinian actually had lots of cash in various accounts in various systems, assuming that the Dominion authorities hadn't snuck in and confiscated it all when he was declared a wanted criminal. Not enough to live on for another hundred years, but a goodly amount.

Nothing in the face of operating costs for *Longshot* and her crew, and that was really his only concern today.

He turned back from his wool-gathering and realized that everyone was sitting around the tents, back out of sight from below and quiet as the grave.

Just watching him.

Captain Tarasicodissa. The man in charge.

Are you people even dumber than I am?

But he didn't say that out loud. He was supposed to be the man with the plan.

The one with the treasure map, which was why everyone was here in the first place. The roguish hero with a lucky streak.

He nodded a good morning to the others as he walked back over there and found a rock that wasn't as chilly as the others from the first hints of morning sun coming over the ridge behind them.

"We good?" he asked Bayjy as he settled.

"All systems clean and responding to remote

commands," she beamed back at him. "And they're all on rotating frequency patterns, so the odds are that none of the muties will even know that there are radio signals floating around. You need a big-ass antenna sticking up from the middle of the village to see that, and they haven't shown that level of technical sophistication or patience."

"Patience?" Kyriaki perked up over the steaming mug of her coffee.

"Signals Intelligence and Decryption is some high-level stuff, Kyrie," Bayjy nodded to her. "Militaries do it, but not many other people. Always a risk those weirdoes down there added militant technophile cult to all the other crap they're accused of. Dave's people would already be all over that, but that sort of craziness is pretty rare around here."

Valentinian actually turned fast enough to see Dave blush, just the slightest amount. That made him feel better, to know that the man was loosening up.

He still remembered the dude who had beat up a bar when they first met.

"What are the radiation counts like?" Valentinian focused on Glaxu next.

As if anticipating the question, he already had his goggles down and was cycling through menu items.

"Based on other studies, Mondi and baseline human have roughly the same susceptibility," Glaxu chirped throatily. "Bayjy is the safest, by design. Given your earlier plans, I do not think we need to return to our ships and clean everything today. We have sufficient water to establish a base inside the ruins and hide it. After that, the pace of salvage penetration will determine how frequently we need to return to the ships, but it would be in our best interests to do so weekly."

Valentinian nodded. That was his other secret superpower. He could juggle all these various options and contingencies as he went, and had recruited a crew of well-balanced experts who would help him execute them.

That included a Mondi science nerd.

"Heads up," Bayjy suddenly barked, looking down at her card-reader intently. "Company on the north approach. Channel nine."

Valentinian walked back to the ridge and stared at the northwestern horizon. From here, all he could see was a thick cloud of dust as what looked like a whole convoy of wheeled transports ripped through the morning sands kicking up roostertails of dust. Bayjy would have better details as she dialed in the magnification, but he took note of the light breeze coming out of the west this morning and made a decision.

"Pack everything now for immediate departure," he said as he walked back to the camp. "Don't worry about pretty right now. I want to use this as a distraction to get us off the mountain during the daylight. The dust will obscure us from below, so I think we can risk it."

Bodies exploded into motion. No questions asked. No arguments. Just an assumption that he knew what he was doing and it would all work out.

Sure. Anything was possible.

Valentinian grabbed the other end of the tent as Dave just collapsed it with bedding inside and they folded it into a laundry-day ball. Tonight would take twice as long to get it set up and organized, plus dumping out whatever grit it had just accumulated, but they were done in thirty seconds instead of ten minutes.

Kyriaki and Bayjy had gone for elegant, at least until they saw what Dave accomplished, and then they joined in. Glaxu had a tarp over a stick, so he was already loading things into the truck.

Less than five minutes later, they were in motion. Valentinian didn't push this morning. Throwing up a dust signature might get someone's attention, but folks in the bowl below them were heading into a pocket sand storm and would be blind when they stopped moving as the winds carried things over them. And a repulsorlift didn't throw up nearly as much crap into the air as wheels did.

An hour later, they were down on the flat part of the valley, parked in what was probably a dry creek bed, if this place still got enough rain to have water flow on the surface. Valentinian figured that it was more likely that most rain never hit the ground, and what did got sucked right down into the sand, unless there was so much falling that a wave of water could carve the stone itself in a flash flood.

Not happening today, so he was in a better frame of mind, down on the flats where he could outrun anything with wheels. Plus he had the three other killers if it came to that.

"What do we know?" he asked as he shut the engines off and pulled out his own card-reader.

Bayjy had not once looked up from her screen during the ride, which was exactly the correct thing to do. The others had the perimeter. She owned the mission right now.

"They're in the big, teardrop square," she replied

after a moment. "Can't gender them from this range, but they don't wear desert robes. More comfortable in the heat, like me. Maybe fifty or so. Guessing a small group of bosses are up on that stage talking or praying, but I've got a mob facing that direction and ignoring the round end completely."

"Make sure to put some audio recording equipment down there where we can listen," Valentinian said. "No idea what language they speak, but it's probably a derivative of Urlan."

"Good idea," Bayjy flashed that smile at him. "I bet their religion would tell us a lot about the city. At least we know where they go, and what time of day to worry."

Valentinian thought about it. They were hidden perhaps ten kilometers away as a vulture flies. Probably half an hour to drive unless he wanted to get crazy, but he didn't want to start cleaning up the mess in the back of the truck if they had to run like hell, so he just leaned back and closed his eyes as they sat in the cool shade and listened to Bayjy's running analysis, like a bizarre sporting event with hilarious color commentary as she made up jokes and belief systems on the fly.

At least nobody had snuck up on them this morning. Tonight, they would put in sensors on the northern approach road, and then they would get to work.

[12]

KYRIAKI

AT LEAST SHE did waiting well. This was a form of stake-out, as far as Kyriaki was concerned. Except that they were waiting for the perp to leave so they could pull a black bag job.

Slip in when someone's not home. Plant necessary electronics around secretly so you can learn their patterns and begin to unravel their lives.

It was never enough to arrest just one person. Life as one of the Dominion Security Bureau's White Hats had taught Kyriaki early on that crime was a game of patterns. Every criminal was eventually connected to other criminals, in addition to all the innocent folks they knew. But you still had to watch the woman that made their coffee down at the corner stand, to make sure that no secret messages were being passed. It was like people watching on a shopping promenade, with the added effort of stopping threats to the Dominion.

Here, she was just making sure everyone was gone before her and her team broke in and robbed the place. Thankfully, her parents would just dismiss their wayward daughter as a revolutionary assassin, and not a common burglar.

"What's so funny?" Vee had opened his eyes and looked up at her.

"I'm going to have to tell people I play piano in a cat house," she said back after a moment, deciding to let the humor stay on the surface for once, instead of being crushed back down deep inside and hidden.

Valentinian's eyes almost crossed in confusion. "Huh?"

"So much better than telling people I rob houses for a living," Kyriaki completed the thought.

"Babe, what do you think a salvager does?" Bayjy sounded indignant now. "You think I introduce myself to people as a woman who robs tombs for a living?"

That generated a mirthful chuckle all the way around the group. How did they end up here?

"*Combat Archaeologist*?" Glaxu dropped the joke in there like a big rock in a small mud puddle and everybody started laughing out loud.

She felt so much better, knowing that everyone else had been wound just as tightly. Maybe she wasn't as crazy as she thought, looking in the mirror occasionally and asking who the hell that woman was.

At least her hair was growing out from the short cut she had maintained in a braid when being official.

"Heads up again," Bayjy's managed to hold her giggles off to one side, never looking up from her screen for long. "Folks breaking up the party now."

Kyriaki checked her card-reader, but didn't bother

opening it. Just the chron on the face. A little under two hours of whatever everyone was doing, so not a revival movement that was going to be running all day and into the night.

Everyone around her sobered, but not that much, from the odd giggles that popped out every once in a while.

"*Armed Field Antiquarian?*" Dave asked in a deadpan tone that nearly caused her to hit her head on the turret ring as she laughed.

It felt good to be home with these people, no matter what happened next.

[13]

IULIANUS

GODS, but he hated this planet. There were no words for the depth of loathing Iulianus had in his heart for Kryuome. At least he didn't have to actually visit that miserable surface this time.

Didn't have to walk about in that stupid heat, threatening anyone and everyone with Dominion firepower if they didn't behave. At least Tarasicodissa had done an excellent job of putting the fear of humans into the natives.

Iulianus still remembered the faint smell of scorched human flesh, which really did resemble roast pig, emanating from the still-smoking ruins of some palace that the rebels had leveled. At least Iulianus had been able to take some professional pride in a job well done, as Tarasicodissa had been training to be a brother officer in the Dominion Armada at one point. And from what the few locals willing to talk, even at gunpoint, had said, that fool Truqtok had had it coming.

But the pirate's death had unleashed a feisty

undertone of racial strife. Iulianus had considered taking off in *Dominion-427* and leveling the rest of the town with energy weapons. Not because he liked the pirates that had been slaughtered, but to remind the smelly aliens that humans were not to be trifled with.

But he was in orbit now. Commanding a true warship that did not land on the surface of a planet. They would need to build the Widow an orbital fortress at some point. Perhaps not as impressive as Dominion Prime, but better than those dumps at Chatosig.

"Time to departure?" Iulianus looked at the supposed countdown clock wending its way to zero.

This wasn't his crack crew that had been able to be relied upon to handle everything before it got to their captain, most of the time. He had many of them. The better ones, too. But he also had a levy of recruits that weren't expecting life to be as sharp on the killing edge as a Dominion warship.

He'd cure them of that soon enough.

"Flight bay reports that they are on track for launch," one of his new officers replied in a carefully-evasive tone that brought Iulianus's head around.

"But?" he asked.

The man blushed.

Seeing human emotion on faces was almost a novel experience. But these weren't Dominion warriors. They were the better dregs of Wildspace.

"If I interpret signals from the flight deck correctly, Captain," the man nodded, almost bowed, as if expecting a blow, "the balinger's crew is still fretting about organization and has not locked everything down internally."

Meaning: the Widow and her gunslinger sidekick

and other killers have disrupted the flight crew with unreasonable demands and not appreciated that Iulianus had hand-picked the pilots he was hiring for those two vessels. That he had hired a blue-skinned Variant Humanity of the Daicia should have told the women how good the pilot was.

He would need to remind her to put her specist tendencies aside if she expected to conquer out here. There weren't that many factory model humans around, especially after all the Urlan geneticists had done when they wanted to pretend to be gods.

Still, nobody would argue with the Widow. He understood that.

"Open a channel to the shuttle," he ordered with a nod of acknowledgement. His bridge crew were better than perhaps he had given them credit for, to have caught things like this and not gotten unbalanced.

"*Warbird-1*. Stassumell here," the pilot replied instantly.

Like they had been expecting his call.

"Put me on your internal intercom, Stassumell," Iulianus said.

"Done."

"*Warbird-1*, this is the bridge," he said baldly. "If you do not detach from the ship in the next eight minutes, you will miss your window and need to wait for approximately four hours until the next time we line everything up. All hands will stow their gear and prepare for orbital burn immediately."

He nodded to the man and cut the line before Athanasia started to argue with him. She might be a fantastic bureaucrat, but this was warfare, and that was an entirely different skillset. He could always fall back on the excuse that he thought one of her gunmen wasn't moving fast enough.

If she chose to take that personally, they could have that argument behind closed doors where only the librarian would know the truth.

But the mission came first.

If Iulianus Palaiologos was going to commit mutiny against his sovereign lord, by all the gods he was going to do a professional job of the thing, damn it.

[14]

BAYJY

AT LEAST THOSE cameras had given her an extra dose of peace of mind.

Bayjy had counted every damned truck and dune buggy that had come in, and then checked them off as they left. If anyone hadn't been aboard and was hiding in the ruins, she hadn't been able to tell, but those fools should have all gone home.

She had planted another set of seismographs on the north road, plus a few in the hinkier areas where she probably got more radiation that was good for the others. She and the T'Brask had the same level of tolerance, so adding a buffer zone around the roads themselves was useful.

And now they were back in town. Down at the south end of things, on the back side of a small hill that might have been a park at some point, or maybe some rich dude's mansion. But they were in the shadow, as far as someone on the road or in that big courtyard was concerned.

The place where they had parked *Longshot*

Hypothesis before would have been bad, if they'd been around for one of these meetings, what Kyrie called revivals. You didn't want to be down in a bowl around here, because rain and wind would accumulate the radioactive metals down there, rather than up on higher places. But you also didn't want to be up where people could see you when they drove up, like the ship had been.

So they were on the south side of the big rock. Brown tarps with mesh had been slung and tacked down to provide shade and protection against wind, as well as concealment from a casual inspection by someone flying in the area.

Wouldn't work if someone happened to come over there, but even on her cameras it was hard to mark the exact spot where the truck had been parked. That was good enough, as long as all those mutie boyz did was come in and sing hymns to each other for a while before leaving.

Captain wanted to hit the place in the latter part of afternoon, so everyone had napped after getting camp set. Glaxu claimed to never actually sleep, so he'd had the watch along with more seismographs and her cameras.

Ain't nobody was sneaking up on them right now.

Night fell slow and kinda leisurely, down here in the basin. Morning were going to be late, since the sun had to climb so high to appear, but right now the sky was bleeding itself out into salmons and pinks before the really good blood colors appeared.

She slung her field bag over her shoulder and set out for a hot date with destiny.

Big Guy had his magic key and a portable toolbox

of surprises with him now. Glaxu and Captain had gone for heavy pistols. Kyrie had turned into the Angel of Vengeance, except this one had smiling eyes, unlike last time.

They were marching through the ruins along the edge of an ancient boulevard that might have once been a canal, long since filled in with sand and dirt. Guns were pointed all directions at all times as they stalked along the edge of the street, including her own plasma rifle that she had been so taken with on her last trip.

Bayjy saw the spot and watched Glaxu scamper ahead on those bird legs of his, claws clicking every time he found stone instead of packed earth under him.

"The way appears clear," he called back a few moments later.

She let him take point. The boys had actually been down here before. She'd only gotten their descriptions later, because they'd forgotten to take pictures of anything except that green stone in the ground.

Rookies.

Big space. Teardrop where they were at the round end, and the muties had been doing their thing down at the point, something like two kilometers away.

Yup, Urlan Late Brutalism architecture on all sides. Probably a High Market from the look, the kind where only the ruling castes were allowed to shop. Peon species would have arcades and underground tunnels in the bad part of town, probably closer to the mountain and away from what had once been a lakefront neighborhood.

Winds had done a number on the place. Ground

at this end looked like a cake that had been frosted, with ripples caused by harmonics, but the sand looked half a meter thick on average.

"Well, crap," she heard Valentinian grumble as he came up beside her. "Last time, it was only about half-covered. Any digging we do now is going to stand out as soon as anyone looks."

"Maybe," Bayjy replied as everyone gathered around to hear her sage wisdom. "And maybe not. Y'all got no idea how easy it is for stuff to seem perfectly flat and hide critters like sheep from any distance."

She eyed the space, rotating it in her head every which way.

"Let's head over to the parking lot," she announced, walking again and letting the others fall into her wake. "There are things we can do over there as well."

Sure enough. Someone liked to drive through here with a dozer blade on the front end of their rig occasionally, pushing piles of sand and crap out of the way and keeping the original cobblestone road at least partly uncovered.

Bayjy walked the parking lot from the moment you came around the corner into the clearing until you parked. Around her, death dealers swarmed like hornets, just waiting for a victim.

Just because it probably mattered, she turned onto the path.

"Time for a little of that old fashioned religion," she laughed as the others groaned.

Urlan religion had been long on droning and racial abuse, and short on redemption for the lesser species, who largely existed as servants, workers, and sex objects. When they weren't food.

She paused and knelt on the path.

"Big Guy, I need your foot here for scale," she simply said.

Dave dropped his heavy boot next to the footprint she was pointing at.

Yup. T'Brask wore boots of some sort. Probable the leather of a local critter, or maybe they traded it outside the wastes.

Whoever had stepped here had a foot bigger than Dave's by about a pinkie toe. Not as wide, though, so maybe designed to run in a straight line, like a Mondi, rather than maneuvering well at speed, like a human could.

If she thought nobody would notice one missing, she might have suggested that Captain bring her a corpse for physical comparison. Didn't want one living, as he could escape and was probably mean enough to run all the way back home to bring friends.

And nobody had anything nice to say about the locals.

Pictures. Pictures. Pictures. High quality scans from her card reader. She had everyone else snapping too, now, just so she could feed them all into a nav computer and let it do the crunching to create a lovely three dimensional map of the place.

Steps up the stage, onto that stone finger stuck out into the crowd for a preacher or a guitar solo, depending on the time of day.

Bayjy memorized the view from the tip and the knuckle, figuring those would be the most relevant.

"What are we looking for, anyway?" Kyriaki's

curiosity finally overcame the complete weirdness of the situation.

"Muties come for a party," Bayjy called back. "We need to be working, and won't have any time at all to bury shit back down when they come, so we need to do it in such a way that it's all hidden from here and there. Invisible, as it were."

"Will it work?"

"I'm carrying a spare pistol in my boot, just in case it don't, beautiful," she grinned at Kyrie and noted the nod back.

Ain't taking us alive, fuckers.

"Vee, can you wander over here?" Bayjy continued. "Need your eyes next."

Captain was wound a little tight, but that had been par for the course since they hit dirt on this planet. Man was nervous that he'd screw something up when it was more than just him and Dave at risk.

Just one of the things she appreciated about the man.

"What's next?" he asked.

Bayjy pointed to a spot on a distant building.

"About there is where you found it?" she asked. "Lined up with that one alleyway?"

He paused and squinted hard for several seconds.

"Further left," he finally decided. "Split the difference to the doorway with the weird gargoyle on the top."

She saw the one he was talking about. Even better, it was more or less behind some of the closer sand and dirt drift piles that had been dozed out of the way.

"Glaxu, need you to head to the parking lot and mark me a spot," Bayjy called.

The Mondi moved like foxes were after him, following the line of her finger as she pointed.

"Little more left. Little more. There!" she yelled. "Mark that spot and we'll join you shortly."

"Adding more dirt there?" Vee hazarded a guess.

"You got it, handsome," Bayjy winked at the man. "Without elevation, the majority of the holes might be anything, but we can hide this one from most of the freaks and hope that the winds don't knock it all down faster than we can build it up."

Dave had joined Glaxu when they got there.

"How wide?" he asked simply.

"Two meters, centered," she replied. "Three would be better."

"On it."

She watched the tall man open his magical tool box and pop out another telescoping baton, like his sword, but this one had buttons to hold it open. A shovel blade appeared and got latched onto the end. Presto, instant shovel.

Okay, that was kinda cool. She might need something like that, if they were going to keep digging up old bones instead of cutting apart dead spaceships.

Big Guy and Glaxu made a weirdly efficient team. The Mondi marked spots with his feet by simply ripping his claws across the ground and loosening the packed soil up while Dave levered liters of soil onto the top of the pile and the back side, forming a platform they could elevate.

Perfect.

Bayjy turned to the other two and pulled them along in her magical wake as she circled the field along the edges of the buildings.

Best to not leave tracks that might not blow away, ya know?

And now, the most awesomest part. Bayjy reached into her messenger bag and pulled out the giant hockey puck Ozzo had sold her. She paced off the distance she wanted and set it down, along with the two marker flags it used to zero the scan field.

She pressed the button and stepped back a few meters, grinning so hard she was afraid her face would freeze like this, just like Momma had always warned her.

The machine trilled merrily to itself and bipped up onto hover mode. She watched it spin in place twice like a hound scenting birds, and then it made a beeline for one edge of the quad, trundling and beeping quietly as it did.

"Now what?" Kyrie asked from close by.

"Now you folk put up some umbrellas for shade and remind the boys to drink a lot of water as they work," Bayjy reached into her bag and pulled out a big towel she had specifically packed for today. "Until the sun goes down, we're going to watch the machine map everything and commit civil engineering."

She smiled at Vee as he suddenly realized what she was up to by laying the towel out and kneeling on it. Shoes came off first, and then shirt.

"And I'm going to get some tan," she grinned as Vee blushed and Kyrie rolled her eyes.

"It is necessary to sunbathe nude?" Captain asked as her shorts joined her shirt, with the card-reader resting atop that so she'd hear beeps and the weight would keep things from blowing if the wind came up.

"Absolutely, Captain," she winked at him as she laid flat on her back, daring him to say or do anything about it as she closed her eyes and prepared for bliss.

God, this felt nice.

Bayjy heard him walk away. Not quite stomping, because that was almost impossible on sand, but he was making a valiant effort.

After a few moments, Kyrie stepped a little closer.

"What do you suppose he would do if I joined you?" she asked quietly.

Bayjy laughed.

"Sunburn his tongue," she chuckled. "Assuming he didn't get a little too involved and end up burning that cute bottom of his instead."

"You are irrepressible," Kyrie chuckled back. "How long will the machine run?"

"User manual says it should have a first pass done in about thirty minutes, give or take," Bayjy let the afternoon sun rub itself across her stomach. "If I wanted to, I could set it on a twelve hour scan, but I'm waiting for that level of detail until after I have the locations of things nailed down."

"You need anything else?" Kyrie asked.

"Pull up one of the folding chairs and flip the umbrella out," Bayjy invited. "As long as you stay out of my sun. Always happy to chat about how easy it is to tease the boys. I doubt Big Guy's even noticed yet."

"And you would be wrong," Kyrie said. "Eyes nearly bugged out, and then he somehow pivoted so he ended up facing this way as he worked. Hope nobody gets hurt over there. At least Glaxu doesn't seem to mind."

"He's probably not as desperately celibate as the other two," Bayjy laughed.

"Got needs?" Kyrie teased.

"Yes, but nothing that can't wait until the next station," Bayjy felt her voice grow a little serious. "I agree with the rest of you that now is not the right time to add something like that to the emotional signature of the ship. But you have no idea how good it feels to get this level of sun on my skin, lady."

"If I had some lotion handy, I might have joined you," Kyrie laughed. "Remember, I was atop *Longshot* nude when you guys got ambushed last time we were here. Considered just putting on boots and an equipment belt to really make the locals nervous when I started hunting them."

"Okay, that would have been righteous to see," Bayjy agreed. "Obviously, we'll need to add a second airlock aft overhead, and a sunbathing platform so we can stay tanned and awesome."

"Sounds good," Kyrie agreed. "First, we just need to make it out of this place, this trap, and find out where we're supposed to go next."

"Agreed," Bayjy said.

Because that was the heart of the matter. Once they did this and got away, what would they want to do with the rest of their lives?

VALENTINIAN

VALENTINIAN MADE a point of standing with his back to where Bayjy and Kyriaki were. Much less distracting to watch Dave and Glaxu add dirt to the pile.

Dave grinned at him when he looked up.

"Don't start, Dave," Valentinian growled.

"I'm just enjoying the view," the tall man smiled and took a long drag of water from a canteen. "If she wants to put on a performance, who am I to argue? Nobody gets hurt."

Above them, Glaxu made a sound that could have been a chuckle as he danced along the dirt, flattening it down and rounding it like the winds had shaped it thus.

Modern art to disguise tomb robbing. Or something like that.

Valentinian rolled his eyes anyway.

"Kyriaki still dressed?" he asked without looking.

"At present, Captain," Glaxu replied, glancing up. "I shall inform you immediately if that changes."

Valentinian shook his head in disbelief and started walking. If nothing else, he could spot for the civil engineers building their little wall. T'Brask were a little taller than humans, according to what Marduk had said, so he would need to maybe hop a little, but if it vanished from his sight, he'd have Dave come over and take a look to see how close they were.

The skies were clear and calm overhead. The blistering sun would set in another two hours or so, bringing the impossible heat down to just annoying, on the way to freaking cold overnight. At least Bayjy would have to get dressed soon.

Hopefully there would be no monsters jumping out at this point, or alarms going off, so that she had to engage in a running firefight naked. Might sound good for a movie, but reality was rarely as much fun in real life.

He spotted the scanner walking its grid in the distance. Noted the locations against his old memories from atop that building over there.

What the hell would someone have buried under here? According to Bayjy, the secret door supposedly under the green stone was unopened, because closing something like that up again afterwards was hard to do. He doubted that winds had filled everything in, especially since the stone had appeared unmolested before.

The rest of the afternoon sky was clear. No birds. No raider ships suddenly swooping down on them.

He pulled his card-reader in a fit of paranoia and checked on *Longshot*, but it was doing fine, hidden out in the open desert well away from any indications of life.

That calmed him. *Longshot Hypothesis* was still

there. Still calmly waiting to carry him away from this planet forever. Hopefully, whatever treasure they did find was small enough to fit in the back of the truck. The alternative would be landing hot and trying to move something with a winch and crane into the bay while maybe fighting off a mutie attack.

He could see why most salvagers preferred to work in space, where there weren't generally neighbors to worry about, and you could always kick in the overdrive for a fast escape if pirates showed up.

Lessons to learn for next time.

Still, he was captain here. He had to suck it up and pretend to be in charge, so he started walking. He could deal with Bayjy being nude. Had seen it before. Same with Kyriaki, if she suddenly decided to join the woman.

Just didn't improve his humor.

The machine apparently decided it was done as he finally walked back over to where the women were relaxing, Bayjy on her towel and Kyriaki in a chair. Even as he approached them, he heard the machine trill once and then return to the starting point and land.

Bayjy had sat up and was studying her card-reader while kneeling. Kyriaki stood to one side behind her, so Valentinian took the other side, able to smell both women's sweat as he did.

This was just one of the reasons he had flown with only Artaxerxes before. The distractions brought by beautiful women.

Still, captain.

He focused on the screen and ignored the view.

"Okay, so we've found the spot to dig," Bayjy suddenly stood and turned to face him.

Standing like this, he stared her about in the nose, since he had boots and she was barefoot. He looked specifically up and smiled expectantly.

"And I should get dressed and act like a professional now, and not a teenage tease," Bayjy completed the thought with a smile.

"That would be helpful," Valentinian agreed.

"Sorry. You go gather up the boys," Bayjy nodded and grabbed clothes.

Valentinian decided the walk would be good. Otherwise, he would be distracted by the reverse strip-tease behind him.

"We there?" Dave was leaning on his shovel.

The wall was perhaps half a meter taller now, but lifted so subtly that it wasn't immediately obvious what had happened.

Hopefully.

"She thinks so," Valentinian joined both of them drinking some more water.

They had a couple of pressurized tanks on the truck, with reminders to keep drinking water constantly. There wouldn't be much peeing in this heat or dry cold, but the brain went weird quietly if you got dehydrated.

All three of them trooped back over to the edge of the field and circled to where Bayjy and Kyriaki had moved. The spot stuck in Valentinian's memory, looking around.

"Okay, we're about above it," Bayjy said, staring at her screen and dancing a little more to her left. "Dig here and make sure to put most of the sand and dirt to the side nearer the stage and parking lot. We'll smooth it out some later, same as the wall, once we have it all out of the hole."

Valentinian let Dave take a watch break and shoveled sand for a while with Glaxu's toes helping. Hard, heavy work, but it focused him on a physical task.

Soon enough, the thunk of metal striking stone. Valentinian climbed out of the current hole and moved his excavations to the side, pulling sand out of the way as it wanted to slide in.

They had debated spraying the surface with something to stabilize it, but Bayjy had decided to wait until they had things done, as the sand would look weird to someone else and draw attention, unless done right.

So he dug. Glaxu scratched like the galaxy's meanest chicken hunting bugs. Dave swapped with him after a bit, since the sand was far harder work than the dirt had been.

Eventually, they had a hole. Scratching at the sides with the shovel, and Valentinian with just gloved hands, they were able to open the edges much faster. As the sun was going down, the gap was six meters across the width and four long ways.

Bayjy stood knee deep and pronounced herself happy.

He was just satisfied that she had gone ahead and layered up for the coming drop in temperatures. They'd be down to probably the low teens by dawn.

"Big Guy, you're on," Bayjy called as everyone stood around and cheered.

Then Kyriaki and Glaxu took up a watch and Valentinian dropped into the hole with the other two. Glaxu would study everything on all the cameras and sensors available. Kyriaki was prepared for watchers.

For whatever brief time such people might continue to exist.

The light was fading, so Valentinian's next job was to set up a couple of lights on tripods they had acquired at Chatosig-Six. Nothing impressive, but they also didn't want T'Brask in the village perhaps wondering about strange lights in the ruins and coming over to investigate.

Dave had a small vacuum that he used to clear off the grit around that big, green planet stone, an emerald perhaps the size of Valentinian's fist.

He wondered if the stone was natural. If it was, there was probably some value to it, but when gems could be created by any industrial press, most of the significance was sentimental. Valentinian was still planning to take it with them afterwards, just to show off later.

The best fish stories always came with a bit of evidence to convince the credulous.

Dave was on his knees, studying the keyhole that the stone represented. Bayjy had marked a spot on the raw stone opposite where Valentinian and she were now standing, as the spot her scanner device had suggested a door would open over there.

Dave made a few adjustments with a couple more tools from the box close at hand and then looked right up at him and smiled.

"Here goes nothing," he said, slipping the five, finger-like tines into the appropriate slots until they stopped moving.

Across the top of the post, Dave added a crossbar with four arms. He leaned his weight into it as

Valentinian watched and cords and veins began to stand out on his arms and neck.

Nothing moved.

"Vee, why don't you give him a hand?" Bayjy asked quietly.

"You're stronger," he noted dryly.

"Yeah, but I need to be watching all the other traps that could open right now," she replied. "You don't know what to look for."

"Gotcha."

Valentinian stepped over next to Dave and grabbed an opposite-side bar, bracing his feet to add torque.

At first, he thought they would need a powertorque in the form of a big drill-press, but something gave way. Slowly at first, as if fighting a last-ditch effort to hold onto its secrets, but two thousand years must have been long enough, because quickly the threads broke free and they were able to rotate the bar through two entire circles before it stopped moving with a thump audible.

"Out of the hole now!" Bayjy barked.

Both men leapt like the planetary crust was opening a crevice beneath their feet.

Valentinian hadn't realized how hard he was breathing, but that was only partly effort, and mostly pure adrenaline from the excitement of the moment.

Since everyone else was armed to some extent, he just turned and squatted at a safe distance as Bayjy oozed her way down into the hole and onto the stone they had been standing on before.

She pulled a light from her belt and shined it into various crooks and gaps, humming to herself.

"Huh," she finally pronounced. "All hands stand by."

Valentinian went ahead and braced his feet. The others rose and drew weapons, so he decided to focus on whatever Bayjy might need, instead of monsters or killer robots that would appear around them.

Bayjy, ever the clown, looked right up at him and winked before putting her weight on the top of Dave's key and pushing straight down. The green planet dropped several centimeters smoothly and then stopped with another clunk.

Nearby, Valentinian saw part of the stone seem to breathe out, for lack of a more descriptive term. Dust expelled, showing a thin crack like a trapdoor.

"Sneaky, rat bastards," Bayjy said aloud as she ignored the key and stepped closer to that spot.

She knelt down and put her nose to the stone almost as Valentinian moved parallel but not too close. She blew on the gap some and ran a thin blade from a multitool that had appeared in her hand.

"We need to clear about a half meter of sand off this side," she stood with a smile on her face as she gestured to the spot. "When we do, the weight on the counter-balance will probably bounce this side right up, so pay attention that you don't get smacked in the face. And we might have to park the truck on top of the hinge if we ever want to close it again. But the sand works in our favor."

"How is that, Bayjy?" Glaxu asked as he stepped close enough to peek over the ledge.

"Normally, something has to pull the door open against the counter-weight," she laughed. "A ton of sand is pushing it down for us, so we can't close it easily instead."

"But that means it maybe has never been opened?" Valentinian asked, finally, possibly, perhaps believing for the first time since that treasure map landed atop a pile of Union Krodageni in a crooked poker game.

"Think so, Vee," Bayjy's grin was serious, but animated.

Like Bayjy, at least some of the time.

"To work then," he said, grabbing the shovel and walking over to where he could start lifting weight out of the way.

Maybe there really was buried treasure down here.

[16]
ATHANASIA

ATHANASIA HAD NEVER BOTHERED LEARNING the history of the region of the galaxy known as Wildspace. The Dominion had been too busy fighting its wars against Laurentia, Asherah, Qetesh, or Lei-Zu to bother with barbaric wilderness beyond any of them.

Oh, she vaguely knew the history of the ancient Urlan Empire that had once covered vast sectors of space. The slow rise. The rebellion. The shattering. *The Darkness.*

But that was about it. The Dominion had figured more centrally.

It was outside the distant fringes of the Urlan Empire that the humans of Cronos had first risen, a warrior cult that would never accept second place. That whole zone was almost exclusively standard human in design, with only a few of the so-called Variants ever encountered.

Still, it was important to know now, so she had spent most of the flight to this system learning about the history of the region and its people from Stephaneria, who had in turn made a study of as much as she could to fill in gaps in her own knowledge.

Out here, in Wildspace, humans were just one of many erect bipeds. Kryuome had at least two other species that were close enough to pass at a distance: Jynarri and T'Brask. The crew of *Phoenix* above her had a few more, although no more M'Rai, pity.

Athanasia looked at a screen showing the view as the shuttle came in to land and imagined that endless sea of tan beneath her as true water, rather than harsh sand and stone. Cronos was a green world, more sea than land, but nothing so boundless as this. She would need to find such a friendly planet as a base, when she was done with these fools.

Or would she?

Jynarri and T'Brask were hard, hardy peoples. Could she tame enough of the desert mutants to conquer softer places? Cronos had turned out brigades of fierce warriors as a cultural thing, but she could see training her own armies in such an unforgiving place as this. Recruiting from it.

She wouldn't probably live long enough to challenge the Dominion itself, but Wildspace recognized no lord save money. How big of an empire could she carve out for herself here?

Athanasia looked over at Stephaneria, the librarian deep in another book. Athanasia was too old to consider having more children, but Stephaneria was not.

She had worked slowly to bring the librarian around to the possibility of Iulianus as a mate. A third generation of power to raise up correctly, so that Athanasia's realm did not die when she did.

All successful empires survive on the basis of bureaucracy. Culture and mores get retained and transmitted thus. Rulers can come and go, but the structure itself survived.

Thus, the Dominion. With a solid backbone of the Solar Party. Rulers chosen by lottery and then combat: intellectual, moral, and finally physical. Only the strongest, the fittest rose, so you never had a weak king.

Yes, she would need to create something like this for her successors. For Stephaneria's children and that generation, if she could convince the woman to accede to the touch of man long enough.

Perhaps Iulianus was merely the wrong one? Athanasia had no doubt what faces burned itself into that woman's torrid dreams. Love and death and hate and orgasm all seemed to be wrapped up into one place. One unknown touch that might cause the woman to become sane again.

Or perhaps shatter her like Wildspace.

Stephaneria looked up, perhaps feeling the weight of Athanasia's gaze. She smiled with warmth. Athanasia reached out a hand that the librarian took and squeezed.

They were both getting close to the moment of their revenge on the men who had wronged them.

"Commander, could you join us on the flight deck please?" the pilot's voice came over the intercom.

Iulianus, of all people, had convinced her to hire a Daicia pilot. She would not have believed a man as specist as Palaiologos would do that, but it was also a measure of how skilled the tiny, blue Variant Human must be.

According to Stephaneria, the species had been engineered by the Urlan as sex objects in the distant past. Smaller than other human species, although not as short as the squat, hairy Viddhu. Sleek and androgynous, regardless of gender. Blue skin and fine, white hair.

All the things, apparently, that caused an Urlan, male or female, to become sexually aroused. Useful to know, as *Phoenix* was likely to travel to places where there were still Urlan-dominated worlds to be found.

Athanasia unbuckled her harness and rose. Stephaneria joined her.

For this mission, she had fallen back on her grays. Body stocking with a tunic and overrobes Stephaneria assured her were critical in the desert, where heat and cold interchanged frequently.

Athanasia made her way out of the crew bay, where her killers passed time reading or sleeping, and onto the forward space, where Stassumell, her Daicia pilot, was strapped in.

He closed the hatch behind them with a finger on his console, and then spun his chair in place.

"Thank you," he said, apparently happy that she had decided to be less rigid than she had been earlier.

Athanasia smiled at him and wondered if Daicia and a human like Stephaneria could be interfertile. Or if it might just be pure pleasure.

"We're hovering at about eight thousand meters ground relative," he said. "All external lights are off and our engines are quiet enough that nobody on the ground will hear us. Additionally, we also are not scanning the ground, for fear of alerting our prey that the jaws are about to close."

"Very good, Stassumell," Athanasia said. "What appears to be the issue?"

The man was competent. Something else must have gone off script.

"As we descended, I was able to detect a spot near where *Longshot Hypothesis* parked last time," Stassumell replied. "Camouflage netting hung to hide something, but it wasn't big enough for that ship, based on what we saw as we were deorbiting."

"So someone is there, but not necessarily Tarasicodissa?" Athanasia asked, feeling Stephaneria tense beside her.

"If it was me, I'd have hidden my ship out in the deep wastes and snuck in," the pilot said. "You mentioned a hover-capable land vehicle, so I'd drive into the ruins and secrete myself. Easier to hide that way. But it might also be someone else, yes."

"Options?" Stephaneria spoke up, unable to contain some emotion.

Possibly rage. Or disappointment.

"Anybody else, and I'd suggest landing at the spot *Longshot Hypothesis* was before as we planned," Stassumell nodded to the other woman. "Nobody but Tarasicodissa's crew would be a match for those killers you brought."

"But those people would be," Athanasia agreed. "Yes, set us down at position three. The walk will be a little greater, but if we come in low from the south, we should be on the ground unnoticed. The wait will be worth it."

"We're not going to raid their camp?" Stephaneria

was suddenly confused, but she was still blinded by her longing to bathe in Tarasicodissa's blood.

Athanasia had never met the man, so she only had the impression he had left on the many others on this quest. Valentinian Tarasicodissa was a highly capable captain with more luck than three men deserved.

"We are not," Athanasia assured both of them. "At least not immediately. After all, there might truly be treasure buried down there."

$$[\ 17 \ ]$$

DAVE

He kept telling himself that it was okay the kids knew he was an architecture nerd. Successful Dominators, like him, got to erect trophy monuments and new buildings. In Dave's case, he had actually helped design about half of them in ways that had surprised the experts he had hired.

We aren't all violence and gore.

So now Dave was envisioning how the trapdoor worked. Simple hinged plate, except that it was a meter thick, two meters wide, and nearly four long. Serious weight was involved, so the pin must be as big around as his thigh.

He had taken the shovel and politely moved the others out of the hole, since Dave figured he had the best reflexes here, not counting Glaxu. Each shovelful of sand got lifted just enough to test the balance point, and then tossed expertly to one side.

Number seven was the magic one. The trapdoor suddenly moved about a handspan upwards as he removed weight. At the other end, the sand settled as the reverse dropped the same amount. He didn't hear any pouring down a hole, so the edges must be pretty trim.

Dave stepped right out onto the trapdoor and it lowered itself to the rest with a thunk.

"What are you doing?" Bayjy asked him almost belligerently.

"Won't move while I'm on it," Dave smiled at her. "Get one of you over here when I clear the other side and we may be able to close it later."

He loved the way her eyes rather crossed as she processed the physics involved. Great thief, but never built a cathedral, that was for sure.

"Huh," she finally said. "Yeah, okay. That might work."

Knowing where the edges were now, Dave moved quickly.

"Vee, you stand on this spot," Dave tapped it with the shovel. "That will hold it down. Kyriaki, maybe you join him, since I weigh more."

Quick enough, both kids were there, standing butt to butt and watching him dig.

Dave cleared the whole trapdoor quickly and stepped clear.

"Both of you step towards me together," Bayjy ordered in a breathless tone.

Dave watched them clear the stone, but nothing moved.

"Okay, good," their thief pronounced. "Big Guy, you push with the shovel very carefully."

He did, and watched the massive stone tilt down away from him as if it was brand new and perfectly lubricated. Those ancients really understood how to build.

Dave joined everyone else on the other side, looking at a set of stone steps descending into the earth.

Bayjy knelt and pushed the stone up and down a little with just her hand.

"Wow," she exclaimed.

Dave watched her stand and very deliberately unhook his key from the green stone and collapse it back down into a series of parallel posts and ends.

"Put this in your toolbox," she ordered him sternly. "Don't want nobody coming up behind us and locking us in."

Dave nodded. He hadn't thought of that. Not that he had any idea who would, but best not to leave the fates with an option.

"Okay, all gear goes with us into the hole, just in case someone comes along during the day," Bayjy said. "Additionally, Big Guy, you stay up here while I look below. If I can close and reopen it, then we'll do that, and hopefully nobody will see anything from up top. Questions?"

How evil and paranoid were those bastards?

But Dave didn't ask that. He'd heard enough about the Urlan. Learned enough, as well. A species that plays with the genetics of others in order to have more efficient slaves doesn't really have any moral or ethical basis, other than perhaps fascism.

Power for power's sake, and nothing more. The only right or wrong was success, by whatever means, whoever's throats you had to cut to get there.

The purple goofball-turned-serious went into the hole with a light in one hand and a knife in the other, chattering constantly to herself. Didn't mean anything, except that everyone could still hear her and knew that nothing bad had happened.

Dave watched the stone pivot from below, and then open again.

Bayjy emerged like Aphrodite in the water.

"Okay, we're golden, at least this far," she grinned at everyone. "Vee, you bring the tripods down. Everyone else clear all your gear and we'll stage it just below here. Then it's back to the camp, sleep, and plan."

"No farther tonight?" Valentinian asked the question everyone else wanted to.

"Nope," Bayjy shook her head. "Don't need much food, but I want to bring the bigger medkit over, and at least one of the tanks of water from camp. Figure we'll need to drive it over, and then lower it with ropes into the hole while it's full. That saves us having to surface as often for water. Underground is going to be just as dry as the surface."

"Oh," Glaxu spoke up. "I am used to my native deserts, where the water table keeps the sands at least somewhat moist underneath."

"Yup, but this is carved into the stone itself," Bayjy nodded. "Maybe they laid down an entire layer instead, but it's dry down here, and dusty. That's gonna suck the water out of you in a hurry."

Dave grabbed his toolbox and carried it into the mouth of the fell beast. Vee had put the two tripods down and aimed them.

There was a room down here. At least of sorts. Three meter ceiling. Maybe five wide and ten long, with a hallway headed in the direction of the stage, at the sharp end of the teadrop, nearly two kilometers away. He wondered how much of this market square had secret tunnels underneath. Useful to escape a slave uprising, since this was the nicer neighborhood close to the hunting lodge palace.

Maybe all these buildings could access this space, and vice versa?

No, if this was for treasure vaults, there would only be a few ways in and out. That's how the Dominator would have done it.

Let the others build their own vaults under their palaces. I shall claim this entire space as mine. Build my vaults here and then cover it over and leave it open.

Dave wondered if all the slaves that had done the work had been executed afterwards to keep the secret. Again, the Dominator might have considered it and the Urlan were far worse.

But someone had survived, so perhaps the slaves had been shipped off-planet with the knowledge. Had drawn a map and passed it to a child, who in turn…

He would never know. But he could probably hazard a better guess on the topic than his friends, as frightening as such knowledge might be.

Quickly enough, everyone went back to the surface and Bayjy had him close the trapdoor. If the winds today were calm, they would not have to dig much when they came back later with the truck.

And then Dave would lead them into the catacombs of the dead.

[18]
IULIANUS

IULIANUS WASN'T PREPARED YET to leave his officers and bridge crew to their own devices for long stretches of time. True, about half had been with him for years, and knew their duty, but the other half were still new to Dominion discipline, regardless of the fig leaf of piracy the ship maintained.

He was a Dominion Armada officer, and this ship would bring whatever glory and honor it could to that name.

So he found himself on the bridge, seated at his small station atop the massive platform that a M'Rai commander had once used to intimidate his crew. Iulianus had considered either chopping it entirely out, or expanding it enough to add two other workstations up here, but in the end had done neither. It let him stretch his legs out and have a small sidetable box installed where he could store things and have a sealed bulb of hot tea on hand.

"Mourouzis," he called to the man currently

responsible for communications. "Status on the ground?"

"*Warbird-1* has landed at one of the alternate locations, sir," the officer replied crisply. "Radio silence since then."

Iulianus grunted, mostly to himself.

He didn't like it. Too much could go wrong, and they would be too far away most of the time to assist.

"Diplovatatzes, have you completed an initial ground scan?" he turned to the woman who handled what sensors a warship like this possessed.

Doing a mapping pass had let them compare to the old one, just to see if anything had changed, and if they needed to do anything about it.

Pirates needed to be ready to raid places with more wealth than security. He didn't see that happening on a shithole like Kryuome, but a good crew acted like professionals at all times.

"One pass complete, Captain," Gordiana replied crisply.

He nodded and turned to the Navigator on duty.

Privately, Iulianus had laughed when some of the new officers and crew came aboard and realized how many of the current crew were female, as if the Dominion held any truck to those silly Wildspace chauvinisms.

No, if Iulianus was going to hate you it would be for your species, not your gender.

Still, the newcomers were shaping up. One of them, a Bahgh woman of all things, had even qualified to serve on his bridge as an officer. A Navigator, no less.

But then, the Urlan had designed the Bahgh as a leader species, smarter than average, and taller, but lean and generally very beautiful. Lower-ranking officers under Urlan commanders, if you will, while brutes like the M'Rai were non-commissioned officers who took orders and cracked heads together.

Brence Rezal wasn't his type physically. Too exotic in her looks, but he had no doubt about her competence, and wasn't looking for a tumble with his officers. There were always strangers on stations if the Widow or the Librarian paled.

He wanted her where she was, teaching the others to overcome their general specism and understand that competence and professionalism earned you points with the captain.

"Rezal, plot us a new orbit," he said, deciding to make some changes while he had this crew on duty. "Above the horizon for where our ground team is, and stable there, but with the best insertion window to put *Warbird-2* on the surface in a hurry."

She studied him for a second with eyes that were too big and the wrong shape, wide and sloped rather than round like he was used to. Fine, blond hair pulled back into a tail, rather than something elaborate.

"Best location will be low, Captain," she said in a flat tone, carefully not challenging his authority so much as offering information for his decision. Yes, she would work out well here. "We cede high orbit to a potential aggressor."

Idly, Iulianus wondered if there were any such threats around here. Certainly, there were pirates in Wildspace. Most transports had some sort of cannon aboard to defend themselves, or relied on speed and evasion.

Phoenix was at least as heavy as anything he had even heard rumors of, operating in the vicinity.

Still, professionalism is a state of mind. A set of habits one learns and then lives.

"Acknowledged, Rezal," he said. "Work with Diplovatatzes and her team to put a probe in a high, polar orbit, looking down on everything and keeping us updated with a laser feed for now. We won't be fighting a pitched battle for Kryuome, nor raiding shipping while we have a team on the ground."

A round of hungry chuckles circled the bridge as the crew understood his implications. Commerce raiding came later. But it would come.

Warships were extremely expensive propositions. Especially big ones like *Phoenix*. They would need to maintain a steady income somehow.

Maybe they would get lucky and find the dragon's horde below them on Kryuome.

[19]

BAYJY

SHE'D BEEN GOOD. Stayed mostly under the tarp and fully dressed all day. Bayjy had even talked Kyrie out of sunbathing, figuring that they'd maybe pushed Vee far enough for one week.

Oh, there had been giggles. Suggestions of wandering out of the shower room nude when the boys were trying to do maintenance on the engines, once they were all back in space, just because they would all be in a new universe once they left this lovely planet.

But Bayjy was being good. That meant making sure everyone else stayed hydrated and took naps during the day. That the vaporators were on and slowly generating water out of the little humidity they could snag, so that the spare tank could go underground later. That all her cameras and sensors were on and not showing anything.

That they were really alone around here.

With nothing better to go on, Bayjy was using the assumption of an eight-day between religious festivals. Or whatever it was the muties did in that market. That was the same schedule that the Jynarri did back in Meeredge and Soulrake, and it was better than nothing.

Plus, she could assume a mid-week event, maybe an evening thing for those folks that could only get halfway without talking to God.

They could go into the ground later today, just as the heat was starting to fade, and have overnight to work. Then they'd take a day off and see if the muties came for tea.

Her afternoon alarm went off with a clarinet trill. Eyes opened and heads turned her way.

Bayjy smiled.

"That's your cue," she said with a slight giggle.

It had taken all four of them to get the water tank into the back of the truck again, but Big Guy and Captain could have probably done it on their own with the set of straps Kyriaki had brought along.

Everybody stretched and looked at the fading, afternoon sky for reassurance, and not just her. Folks were too serious today, but she understood.

Salvagers frequently got a little morbid and maybe depressed when they got right up to the point where they were going to open up the treasure vault. Something about the actuality not ever being anywhere near as good as all the dreams, and you had to settle for living in the real world.

Only once had she looked at true avarice, standing in the middle of that Urlan Sanctuary, and understanding what something like that would be worth to the right collector.

Before Butler screwed her and all her friends out of their own personal dreams.

On the one hand, it was too bad that he was dead now, and she'd never get her own personal revenge on the man. On the other, Glaxu had kicked his stupid ass alone, which had to have been all the more galling, to have a wee, little Mondi take you down.

Sucker was dead. Never hurting anyone, ever again.

Maybe one of these days, she'd go and try to find Mitch and the others, just so she could return all their memories to them. All the things Butler had stolen when he backed away from the station without any warning.

Captain mounted up without a word, but he was in the serious zone right now, and didn't need her and Kyrie goofing around and teasing. Glaxu had perched on the truck all afternoon, squatted down like it was a little nest where he could see a greater distance.

Big Guy handed her up into the bed of the truck like a Dominion Lord taking his lady to a ball, but he could be like that. Kyrie didn't bother, just hopped up and brought her death guns live.

Everybody dealt with stress their own way.

She checked all her cameras and sensors as Vee started back to the site. He and Glaxu would come back here with the truck once they got the water unloaded, and then return on foot while she inspected the tunnels for that next trap some asshole Urlan architect would have had to add.

It was like they had it in their DNA or something.

Hot sun. Hot breeze. Still skies empty of everything.

It would have been nice if Kryuome still had a moon, but apparently blowing that tiny rock to hell had given the humans the ammunition they needed to bombard the surface.

Lesson there, bubbles. Never make humans angry. We'll blow up your damned moons to rain fire on your planets and wipe your stupid ass off the face of the galaxy.

Nothing moving in the hollow ruins of T'Ilard, save the tomb raiders driving to the scene of the crime. It was weird being on a planet with so few birds, but Bayjy supposed that all the radiation would kill a bunch, and the desert didn't leave much for anybody else to eat. At least there were vultures and stuff closer to Meeredge. Maybe eventually the desert would stop glowing at night and flying things would be able to spread back out.

She'd be long gone by then, but the folks in town weren't all that bad.

Guns, guns, guns. That was her life today.

Nobody jumped out to commit suicide so they drove right up next to where she'd closed up the tunnel. Captain parked, Big Guy opened the trap door up. Glaxu ran a fast patrol lap around the outside, but he might just be showing off at this point.

He was like that.

And just like that, they had fifty gallons of fresh, pure water in a pressurized tank down in the tunnels, along with enough food for a month, as long as they found someplace to stash poop.

"Back in ten," Vee said as he and Glaxu headed back to the camp.

"How do you want us?" Kyrie asked, glancing at Dave.

"One of you down in the hole with me," Bayjy replied. "The other at the top of the stairs keeping watch for looters, muties, and archangels with trumpets."

Bayjy descended the stairs with Kyrie close at hand. Probably a better bet, since Big Guy still had that cannon of his. The lights down here were on and bright. Batteries would run for at least a month, so she had left them running.

Carved stone when she touched it. Dave had talked about whether it was made by slaves, cut into the surface, or poured like concrete. Touching it, this looked like the top of a volcano that had been cut with high-power beams. Sectioned out and then carried away on sleds or wagons. Overhead was solid, so the surface embellishments the boys had talked about had been added over that like frosting.

"You stand right here," Bayjy pointed to a spot where Kyrie could see down the hallway, and shoot if she had to, but wasn't going to set off any dumb traps.

Stupid Urlans.

Bayjy didn't know what she was afraid of, but wanted to be prepared for anything. Could the Urlan make a killer robot that would still be working after this long? Anything living would have died out, or evolved into something else by now.

She knelt in line with the entry to the hallway but nowhere near it.

Just how mean was this bastard?

Ozzo had sold her a couple of other toys, when he basically gave her the one that let her map most of this section of tunnels. She aimed one at the doorway and turned it on.

No electronics of any kind. Not surprising. Could have been at one point, but batteries would die.

Unless someone built a charger into the floor or walls that could react to spotlights and convert that to electricity. Both mean and subtle.

And why she'd left the lights on all night.

There was a power source in the doorway, all right.

Photo-sensitive paint, maybe? Probably.

If I was going to do something like that, I'd assume that they made it past the doorway before it got enough charge, so they'd be emerging with whatever they stole from me. So I put an eyebeam in the chokepoint and then do something nasty. There will be more than one invader most likely, and I have them trapped back in that hallway. Do I drop a wall, or flip the floor out from under them?

"How could you move that much floor to get everyone?" Kyrie asked.

Bayjy realized she'd been muttering to herself instead of inside. Or thinking really loud, there was always that. She looked up at Kyrie and blushed.

Which was saying something, as lavender as she already felt.

"I'm an Urlan son of a diseased camel, so I want to gloat over people I caught stealing my stuff," Bayjy still just talking out loud. "Maybe I pivot the floor out from under you and drop you into a pit, and then close it up again afterwards. The scanner showed levels of depth under here, but just hollow spots and stone, so I can't tell what their purpose was."

"Would it work?" Kyrie asked, gun still pointed down that long hallway.

"Probably," Bayjy nodded for both of them. "Put the hinge point back a little ways from the wall, so the center of gravity is off. Charge the machine to pull a pin out and let it go."

"How do we disarm it?" Kyrie's voice got concerned.

"We kill the battery and hope," Bayjy reached for another device in her messenger bag. "Don't know where the magic switch is to just turn all the security off, but I'm going to assume every door is trapped until I do."

She looked at the stone around her, but it appeared to be solid.

"You move onto the stairs, just in case," Bayjy suggested.

Once Kyrie was clear, she aimed a small cutting laser at the spot on the wall and smiled when a large chunk of paint suddenly blackened. Wiring melted the paint close by the impact point.

A few moments later, the battery failed with a pop and a puff of smoke.

And nothing fell out from under her, dropping her sorry ass into a pit for the boys to come rescue.

"Next, a little insurance," she called, pulling out a coil of rope and putting on some gloves. She handed one end to Kyrie and reached a foot past the doorway and put some weight on the floor. Nothing gave. And no rocks fell out of the ceiling on her, either.

Never know what those Urlan bastards might have done.

"We good?" Kyrie asked as Bayjy came back out of the hallway.

"I hope so," Bayjy said quietly. "I'm expecting more traps, but can't tell you how many of them have failed from entropy. We'll move slowly and carefully, and treat every door as a bomb for now, but I think this room is secure. At least once I scan everything from down here."

Bayjy took a deep breath and pointed Ozzo's scanner at the doorway again. Nothing registered as a power source which was as good as she could do now. Primitive traps would be a risk, but the Urlan had to have had a way to get around things, and they would have powered things. Like that stupid door.

She turned slowly to her right, looking for anything that might spell trouble.

IT WAS good that she had instructed the pilot to land at one of the alternate points. Athanasia saw one of her hired men signal everyone to be quiet and for her to join him.

The shuttle was parked down in a small gully of sorts. Out of sight until you were right on top of it, which was good. Her man had a decent enough view of where the other camp was, off in the middle distance.

Athanasia felt Stephaneria's presence and they both crept to the top of the hill, next to a shattered wall that time and winds had brought down. The gunman pointed and she saw a hover vehicle pull into the covered area. A moment later, Tarasicodissa and that turncoat Mondi emerged on foot, heading back the way they had come.

Athanasia glanced around and confirmed that the setting sun was more or less behind them, which would help with stealth, but there was just so much open space around here, in spite of all the ruins and piles of rubble and sand.

"Two of you stalk them to the rest," she said to the man. "Then lead us to where they are."

Others had gathered below them, hidden. The gunman nodded to the man the others normally considered the next leader behind the two women, an old, grizzled veteran who still moved on utterly silent feet when he wanted to.

Athanasia watched as he nodded two others into motion interestingly, one of them was female, which was rare. She was the only other female in this group.

The two moved like ghosts as she watched from cover.

Tarasicodissa and Redtip were not making any great effort at stealth themselves, nor watching their back trail, so they must feel like they were alone. She wondered what systems the man and his crew might have set up to watch for trouble, but didn't have time to locate them.

If the two were leading her killers into a trap, she would just have to make sure that they were as toxic as possible. And that Iulianus was ready to come to her rescue, should she need it.

"Everyone else strap it up and prepare to move," the man she thought of as Force Leader spoke up now. "Water and rations for two days. Cache the rest here, as the shuttle will depart on schedule?"

That last he said as he was facing her for confirmation. Athanasia nodded. Their shuttle would depart as soon as full dark had fallen, just on the off-chance than he had not been seen, and could get away in the shadows.

Athanasia had a pistol and a sword that she

added now, strapping on a bandolier to hold them, with the small backpack she had insisted on, in spite of being in command. Medkit, food, a soft-sided canteen. The basics of desert survival. Stephaneria had the same, except she wasn't bringing a sword to what might be a gun fight.

Athanasia would never go into battle without the weapon she had trained on for fifty years.

Quickly enough, the remaining ten of them moved out in a column, with her and the librarian in the middle for safety. The sun was just above the horizon now, so they would need to move with some speed, just so they didn't have to have lights out.

There was no moon overhead to provide light to hunt by, so they needed to be in position quickly.

Force Leader followed the trail marked by the other two, and quickly enough Athanasia found herself at the edge of a large market square, or something similar. Her first two killers were in place at the edge, watching from inside a ruined brick mansion of some sort, from the few interior decorations that time had not erased. She joined them just in time to watch a light disappear from the middle of the space.

It was as though a door had closed, but there was nothing there. Trapdoor? In the middle of the sidewalk?

What an utterly gauche thing to do.

But these were Urlan. Nothing Athanasia had heard about the species had particularly impressed her, save for perhaps their ruthlessness, which approached the standards of the Dominion.

"Commander?" her sergeant asked.

"Send the scouts," she decided. "But 'ware an ambush."

Those words caused the men around her to go into high-hostile-mode, guns sniffing for movement and risk.

The two scouts crept carefully from cover and approached. Stephaneria had located some electronic lenses somewhere and was studying the courtyard silently. Athanasia leaned out just enough to watch.

There was a hole out there, apparently. The male scout dropped waist-deep and looked around before signaling the others. Half the team followed, but she kept Stephaneria here for now.

This was just about as perfect a spot for an ambush as she could imagine. Let the others die if it was. She checked in her belt for the emergency communicator she and Stephaneria carried. Iulianus was a few hours away, at worst. Sooner if he had loaded up the shuttle and was hovering it at a low orbital elevation.

That he had thrown his lot in with her gave Athanasia some solace. He was as trapped as she was, but apparently just as willing to go pirate and carve out his own glory with her assistance. And he was pleasant enough in bed, though she would need to test the Daicia's designed abilities at some point.

The team were using short-range comms to talk. Encrypted and secure. She wasn't on the loop, because they spoke almost their own language in the field, but the Force Leader seemed relieved as he listened.

"Trapdoor in the middle of nowhere, Commander," he murmured now. "Team assumes some sort of catacombs beneath us."

She turned to her expert with an inquisitive look.

"That would fit an Urlan facility," Stephaneria confirmed after a moment. "This was a city at some point, so probably it had a palace not far away. This courtyard would assure the rulers of security, since others would only be allowed to dig their own vaults down."

"Treasure vault in the middle of the open city?" Athanasia was appalled.

"The Urlan are aliens," her librarian nodded. "They look human externally, but that's all. And their culture was brutality distilled, with human kept as slaves and pets. Arrogance."

Yes, she understood that concept. *You can't stop me, so I shall do whatever I wish.*

Her former husband, the man everyone knew now as Dave Hall, had been that way when he was younger, before age and experience had tempered him into one of the better Dominators in the last two centuries. Not one of the giants of the early era, who had created the Dominion from scratch and then conquered hundreds of worlds, but he had expanded more than several of his predecessors.

Now she just had to take it all away from him.

"Stephaneria, will our comm signals get through any depth of stone?" she asked.

"Some," the woman replied. "I can't be sure until we're beneath and try."

"So it might be a trap, designed to isolate us entirely from help?" she asked.

Stephaneria shrugged.

Athanasia pulled out her personal comm and brought it live.

"Palaiologos here," Iulianus responded immediately.

"We are about to enter an underground vault of unknown depth and provenance," Athanasia said simply. "We may be unable to get a signal to orbit through the atmosphere."

He paused for a second, obviously considering his options, even as hers became constrained.

"I will take the second team and move to the ground nearby," he finally said. "That way we can be close if you need assistance."

"Very good, Captain," she smiled. "Mark these coordinates and prepare."

She closed the comm and replaced it. Ionospheres were always tricky, especially when you added stone. But if he was below that, the signal should be readable.

One less thing to worry about.

She nodded to the Force Leader and he got everyone into motion, a porcupine ready to go defensive at the first sign of a bobcat. She and Stephaneria moved in the center of the storm, untouched but protected.

Tarasicodissa's famous treasure map had led him here, to a hole dug in the sands of Kryuome and a trapdoor into the catacombs of T'Ilard. She felt like a lord with a mastiff straining at his leash, dragging her across the galaxy after some treat, but they had arrived.

"Options?" she asked the Force Leader.

"I would suggest time for them to move beyond the doorway, if you want to take any alive," the man replied. "We could open it and chuck explosives down there easy enough, but you would probably not find recognizable parts. Alternatively, they might react if the door opens while they are right there, and lob detonators out at us."

"Give them time," she decided.

She might as well let her hound find whatever treasure could be here as well. She could be patient.

Beneath her feet were the fugitives she had chased so far. Valentinian Tarasicodissa, rebel captain. Kyriaki Apokapes, rogue Security Bureau officer. Redtip, the double agent who had killed Vidy-Wooders.

And Dave Hall. She would not address him with that other name. He had forfeited his right to it when he faked his own death to escape her. To cast her out of power and glory and force her to start from scratch, surrounded by fools, misfits, and aliens.

Yes, she had a special vengeance planned for that man.

Soon, Dave Hall. Very soon.

[21]
VALENTINIAN

IT WAS like descending into the stomach of a whale, but Valentinian had already steeled himself for it. He'd spent the last several years being in space in a small starship, so he wasn't sure where this level of discomfort about being underground came from. Maybe it was just the feeling of all that rock above him that weighed on his soul.

He had closed the big trapdoor, wiggling it once just to make sure that he could move it from underneath alone if he needed to later. No panic there, not at all.

The others were waiting for him when he turned back and took a deep breath.

"Okay, so I disarmed the second trap already," Bayjy shone a light on a spot where the wall was scorched. He could smell traces of smoke in the still air. "There was a battery there that would have set something off. Not sure what, but don't open any door or go through any archway until I check it. Are we clear?"

Valentinian agreed along with everyone else. He would have never have considered doing something like this operation without her as an expert. Probably would have just framed the map and hung it on the wall in his room or something.

But he was here, now, doing this thing. He had an expert, and he would listen to her. Simple as that.

No panic at all on his part.

"Okay," Bayjy nodded fiercely at everyone. "Now I'm going to lead, and I'll have a length of rope tied around me, in case I miss something and start to fall. Big Guy, your job is to catch me. Glaxu, you'll test small places where your weight might not set things off. Vee and Kyrie, if it jumps out, kill it and then ask questions later. We good?"

Again, the assent. He could do that. The stress of walking down here would have him on edge enough that NOT drawing and shooting something jumping out would be the hard part.

He had no doubt that Kyriaki would be on point with her assault pulsar.

He found himself at the tail of the column as they moved. If he had to say so, he thought the floor was slanting slowly down as they moved. Barely noticeable, but it might roll a marble. The floors weren't polished smooth, but a two-centimeter ball bearing would do the trick if he had one.

He had a light in his off hand, same as everybody else. The walls were a weird color somewhere halfway between green and gray, like something a cat might hack up if they decided to become a painter. At least the air didn't smell the same.

Another reason he didn't have a cat aboard *Longshot*.

"Okay, first checkpoint," Bayjy's voice floated back to him.

Valentinian turned sideways so he could watch both directions. Kyriaki did the same from across the way, so they were almost looking at each other, except they just swapped views constantly.

Forward. Back. Forward. Back.

Whatever Bayjy was doing involved a little bit of humming to herself followed by drafts of silence and the odd curse. Must be good.

The air down here wasn't as stale as he was expecting for being abandoned for millennia, so he assumed that a chimney came out somewhere. Possibly rocks fallen in or something. Hopefully they didn't dead end in a rock fall.

Bayjy had stopped at a door. From the way it echoed under her knuckles, some sort of solid core panel, but a polymer of some sort rather than wood or steel.

"Okay, door is about to open, everybody put a bottom against a sidewall and look for movement anywhere," Bayjy called.

Valentinian faced aft and prepared for something coming down those stairs back there. They must have moved a couple hundred meters from where they'd started, he thought, but the tunnel wasn't straight so it was hard to tell. Soft curves back and forth, but he couldn't decide if they were artistic or designed to keep surface light out.

Who knew what Urlans considered good design aesthetic? Especially considering the stuff on the surface.

Sound of a door opening. Maybe a hint of a breeze headed forward, but he couldn't be sure.

"Breeze?" he asked, figuring it was better safe than sorry.

"Noted," Bayjy called from her end. "Headed downhill with us, so maybe a little bit of a seal on this door."

"Roger that."

No lights appeared behind him. No sounds of the boogieman coming this way. Just tons and tons of angry, grayish rock overhead, waiting for the chance to leap out and squish him if it got the opportunity.

Valentinian shook his head in something of disbelief and focused on the real world, and not the fingers of claustrophobia plucking at his soul.

He'd be in space soon enough. Endless, empty space.

Bayjy was kneeling down and peeking through the door when he looked, holding a scanner in one hand and a light in the other. Glaxu had a gun.

And Dave Hall *was* a weapon.

"Okay, I'm not relaxing, but we seem to be inside the security perimeter for now," she called. "This door had some sort of mechanism, but it shorted out so long ago spiders have colonized it and I can't detect any power signals. Moving slowly forward."

He looked, and she was holding the door open with one hand and stringing her thin line underneath.

"Closing the door, Dave," she said. "Glaxu, you be on my side just in case."

They did, and he found the space darker all of a sudden. Not black, just two lights shorter than it had been.

An endless moment passed, and the door opened again.

"I knew those bastards couldn't just do one," she growled as she scanned. "Stand by while I disarm another trap that only activates when the door opens and closes."

Valentinian had no idea what she was doing, but he didn't sense any stress in her voice beyond the angry admiration of an Urlan security sadist dead for twenty centuries and still giving her grief.

The door remained open when he glanced, but Bayjy was facing this direction, working on the handle side of the sill.

Something popped angrily with a few sparks and then faded to just Bayjy cursing fluently in Urlan. He knew enough of those words to follow.

She was deeply pissed.

"Okay," she announced finally with a huff. "Look for mechanisms on the doors that release a weight when it opens without the right key. Son of a diseased camel is using those to fast charge batteries. It was like he knew I was coming and everything else would fail by now."

Valentinian nodded. He'd assumed that his map had led others here looking for buried treasure. The T'Brask wouldn't have gotten them all, but if you went in assuming that age would defeat everything and it would be a cake walk, you probably ended up at the bottom of some pit, dying of thirst or lack of air, depending on how tight it sealed up on you afterwards.

But she moved them all through the door and closed it behind them slowly and carefully. Valentinian looked and saw a spot where a thin bar stuck out of a hole. Heavier than wire, but not much. Probably exactly the thing you put in to block something while arming your trap, so it didn't go off on you.

Everything in here had changed from outside. The floor underneath was suddenly a gorgeous mosaic tile of some enchanting scene he assumed was this planet, back when it was green, and Urlan lords hunted game on the equivalent of horses. Or something.

The walls showed designs where columns had been erected, or not cut out, and then plated over with something a silvery color that hadn't dulled or corroded, even with what little humidity the air had. Even the air smelled better, somehow.

The walls had also pulled back some. Instead of a simple hallway, maybe three meters wide, this was ten or more wide, and vaulted to nearly five meters height. They must have gone down a ways without necessarily realizing it.

Him, anyway. Dave, Glaxu, and Bayjy probably had it measured to the centimeter. Kyriaki, too.

Valentinian looked up and realized part of what made him feel better. There was light in here. Weird and subtle, but light.

He saw massive quartz stones that had been set in the ceiling and were letting sunlight in. Wild. And the ceiling was so high that it wasn't about to crush him.

Okay, so I'm never taking a job in a mine. Good to know.

Bayjy drifted to her left, and the crew followed.

There was a hole over here. No, a pool or something. Dry and covered with a tiny layer of dust, but more decorative than anything. You could wade in it and not get your belt wet, plus it was kinda roundish.

After a moment, the image came clear.

"Fish pond," he said out loud without meaning to.

"Huh," Bayjy grunted back. "Think you're right, Vee. This may have been an underground grotto for lunch or something, like the surface above us."

"I thought we were looking for treasure vaults or something?" Kyriaki spoke up.

He glanced over at her and she smiled. No panic from being underground in that woman.

Or probably anything else. Just him.

"There are doors," Glaxu gestured with one toe in a sweep.

Valentinian looked around the room and his heart stopped.

He must have said something, because Dave suddenly cut off all light and vision in front of him.

One big hand was holding him upright, although he couldn't remember falling over. Must not have hit the floor.

"You okay, Vee?" Dave asked.

Valentinian shook his head to knock things loose. Or back into alignment. Something.

The others were gathered around him as well. He could read concern on all their faces.

"What happened?" he asked, hoping no rocks had jumped out and bit him when he wasn't looking.

"You said something that would have gotten my mother to wash your mouth out with soap," Bayjy smiled carefully at him. "Then started to wobble. Would have face-planted in the duck pond, but Dave caught you. Held you there for a second and then you came back from wherever you went. Where were you?"

Valentinian nodded. That made perfect sense. Completely insane, but perfect sense.

Without trying to brush Dave's arm off, even if he thought he could, Valentinian pointed at the side wall on the right. The thing that had caught his eye.

Yup, clockwise. Stupid Urlan could never settle for just one joke on everyone.

"Look familiar?" Valentinian asked everyone.

A green planet had been set into the wall with mosaic tiles. Against a background so faint he wasn't sure you could still call it green. He needed a painter to tell him the color code for that.

"You good?" Dave asked.

"Think so," Valentinian replied.

It was as much the truth as anything. And Dave stayed close after letting go of his arm.

Bayjy led. Even whatever fuzz had just colonized his head wasn't going to convince Valentinian to walk over there ahead of the woman who would be the one saving his ass, most likely.

"My key won't fit anything here," Dave said aloud soberly.

"Don't need to," Valentinian heard himself say. "The planet rotates clockwise."

"Are you shitting me, Vee?" Bayjy grumbled.

He pulled out the map from the pocket where he had it stowed and opened the waterproof bag that protected it. Unfolded it enough to show the stack of coordinates. Showed her the bottom row, a set of Urlan hieroglyphics that had confused the hell out of him for so long.

"That no good, dirty, low-down, motherless, son

of a…" Bayjy rattled before fading into an inarticulate growl. "Everyone stand well back while I look at it."

Valentinian suddenly felt like he was helium-filled, so he kept his mouth shut. The light bounciness was fine, but the squeaky voice would just ruin everything right now.

He smiled at the ceiling instead.

Bayjy fiddled. Everyone else watched. Valentinian kept his eye on the door they had come in, because that was his job. He could just envision a squeaky mouse calling an alert.

Dear God, don't let them cast me as a mouse when they make this whole thing into a children's cartoon…

More grumbling. In at least five languages, if he was following Bayjy's mood.

Finally, she just put both hands on the planet and used the friction of her palms to turn it. Even from over here, he heard something click.

"Vee, you have obviously been blessed by the gods, so remind me to never play poker with you, ever again," Bayjy called.

"You'll get bored," he laughed back.

"Okay, never for real money," she answered.

Everyone chuckled. Poker for fake money had been how this all started. Well, not fake, but Union Krodageni weren't worth nearly that much, compared to Dominion Solars, so he'd been mostly playing for fun. And lunch money.

She'd been in over her head trying to build a stake, and had lucked into two sharps, not one. Lucky for her, she hadn't been the mark.

And it had all turned out pretty good, so far.

"Come see what you've done to me, you lucky

skunk," Bayjy stepped to one side with a grand, theatrical flourish.

The wall moved.

What was it with Urlan designers and huge stones balanced perfectly on hinge pins? This wasn't pseudostone made to look real. No, this was a chunk of marble or granite or something off-gray, polished and tiled on one side, and thirty centimeters thick. Thing must weigh a ton. Yet Bayjy moved it with one hand.

Valentinian looked into a newly revealed hallway. Then he looked down and realized that another pond mostly kept pedestrians from walking here, as Bayjy was on a space about half as wide as a sidewalk that ran between the pond and the wall.

He could see piles of something, now that he looked, where what he guessed were railings had rusted and collapsed.

Man, just how far gone was he? Good thing he had the others watching, he might have tripped on one and face-planted.

Except, looking back, he had unconsciously stepped right over one and never processed it.

Valentinian kept the curse words inside this time.

"So what's back there?" Kyriaki asked instead.

"Maybe your vaults," Bayjy shrugged.

They fell back into inspection mode, but the woman couldn't find any traps here. Maybe the fish pond was enough to keep the casual person at bay?

And they were underground, in a secret space to begin with, and you'd have to know about the planet on the wall and what to do with it.

And. And. And.

Valentinian took a deep breath and followed the

others as they entered another dark corridor. Except it wasn't that dark. Just not as bright as the big room. Still had quartz in the ceilings, but set every once in a while like overhead lights.

Except it was night upstairs. There shouldn't be light.

"Bayjy, where is the light coming from?" he called in a concerned voice. "Sun's down, right?"

Ye Gods, had they fallen into a fairy tale and time was moving at a different rate?

"You missed that part I guess," she said. "The stone is a kind that absorbs light and heat all day, and will glow until it cools down. Except as much stone as they have here, that's probably measured in days, so it just stays at the same brightness all the time."

"Do I want to know how it works?" he asked anyway.

"No," Bayjy said. "I mean, if I told you photosynthesis for rocks, that's probably good enough for now. This stuff is actually a hardened polymer foam, not real rock. And the background radiation count down here is actually lower than most planets, but I'm guessing that the stuff absorbs it even better than the sunlight. Plus it's been sealed, so we're probably bringing stuff with us."

She'd been right. He didn't want to know that badly. It made even less sense, unless someone could somehow replicate it and have a rock that glowed forever if you kept it warm and bright. Not useful on a starship, he was guessing, and most planets would probably get a little pissy if you told them it was Urlan science.

Yeah, we'll just let that one go for now.

This corridor curved like all the others did. Must

be an Urlan thing, because Valentinian couldn't think of another culture that wouldn't do straight lines underground.

At the end, another door. Another trap. And Another Trap. AND Another Trap.

That bastard was earning his time in hell, from Bayjy's running commentary.

Then she opened the door at the end of the corridor.

Based on previous conversations, her own mother would need to wash her mouth out with soap.

Valentinian entered last. And just added himself to the line of people awaiting Bayjy's mom.

This was a hangar. Didn't matter what they had done to the walls to shape them round instead of square. Or the strange shelving units that looked like they had been grown out of those walls. Or the spaces that looked like offices and such, on this floor and a catwalk running around things to his left.

Because the thing in front of him was a ship.

An Urlan starship. Sitting here like a hound taking a nap, curled up in front of his dad's fireplace on a cold day.

"Vee, tell me I'm not dreaming," Bayjy finally reverted to a language fit for the evening news.

He followed her out into the room. Chamber. Hangar.

They were in a bubble of space two hundred and fifty or three hundred meters long. Forty or fifty high. Seventy wide.

With an Urlan starship squatting in the middle of it.

Except squatting was the wrong term. That

suggested something as ugly and brutal as Urlan architecture in the city above them.

He wasn't even sure the same species had designed this elegant bird.

Longshot Hypothesis was, like most ships, generally a square tube with pieces welded on. The wings on the front with the engines in his case. *Outermost* folded up like a utility knife when it was on the ground.

This was art. Tall and skinny like a wading bird. Smooth, flowing lines and curves. Rounded everything, with spaces where the engine nacelles and lifters were exposed by open plates, as well as the landing gear.

He had an image of a giant log that had been washing around in sea and storm for years, slowly eroding into smoothly sculpted lines that made *Longshot* look ugly. And she was the most beautiful ship in space.

From a distance, the ship had a bird's crest at the front, like three, narrow decks atop the bridge. It almost reminded him of a carpenter's hammer he had stashed away in a toolbox, with a long, rounded body that came to a head with a narrow deck down on tiny landing feet and that head up.

Behind that, over the engine and machinery area, was another fin, but it was maybe one deck tall and only a few meters wide and maybe five long. Valentinian couldn't imagine what purpose it served.

He had never seen anything like it for a design.

They were all underneath now, cursing and whispering like they were in church in their best clothes.

Valentinian ran a hand along the hull metal and

shined his light up to confirm it. The metal was two colors, steel gray with swirls like a fancy cake, done in something softer than red and darker than orange.

It should look hideous, but it was gorgeous. He ran his hand across it again and the hull felt almost more like plastic than anything, so he wondered if it was metal at all, or some ancient Urlan technology that had gotten lost.

"Vee?" Dave asked from close by.

"Bayjy, is this real?" Valentinian in turn asked her.

They were all in a tight cluster now, like a flock of birds seeking comfort and solace from one another.

He could only imagine the value of an ancient, Urlan vessel still in this good of a condition, at least externally.

"I think so, Captain," she replied, which told him how weirded out she was, to call him anything but Vee.

He turned and looked at the bow. That hammerhead bird crest that went up and down, unlike the shark going side to side. There was a short set of stairs that led up to a hatch.

The whole ship measured fourteen meters wide or so, just eyeballing it. Two engine pods came off the rear, but this didn't look like a cargo vessel at all.

High-speed transport, maybe. Maybe someone's personal yacht. The style spoke of speed and elegance.

"What would cause it to be here, and not elsewhere?" Kyriaki spoke up.

She was probably the only one here not currently mentally diving into pools of gold coins, like that one cartoon character.

Always a cop.

"I mean, the war came here and they were nuking the planet at the end, right?" she continued. "Why didn't they leave?"

"I would guess, Kyriaki Apokapes, that they died on this planet, having fled here from elsewhere, and the secret of their ship died with them," Glaxu stood up to his full head crest height.

Valentinian had to nod with that. Kryuome had died around them two thousand years ago under nuclear fire and bolide bombardment.

"Bayjy, would we find anyone aboard?" Dave asked, head still rotating constantly like he was expecting someone to come after them.

"I have no idea, but we're going to treat this like everything else," she replied. "A trap until I say otherwise."

Valentinian moved to one side, where he had a nice view of this giant, predatory bird, and watched. He could just smell trouble coming.

"Confirm that," Iulianus said, speaking to Martinianus Rendakis, back up on the bridge of *Phoenix*, above them in orbit.

"We confirmed before we opened a signal, Captain," the man said, his normally bland face taking on seriousness on the screen. Were all his old officers suddenly coming to life, infected by the piracy bug? "We're picking up all manner of activity at the settlement right now, including previously-undetected radio signals."

"What are they saying?" Iulianus asked.

"We don't speak the language, sir," the current First Mate replied. "But the tones are angry and seem to be almost a war cry. A summoning of the clans, since others are responding on the same channel from more distant locations. None of them are close enough to reach you any time soon, but we've got cameras zoomed in as tight and as stable as we can, and there are lights coming on around the one facility. Again, previously undetected."

"Have *Warbird-1* load up with more combat troops," Iulianus ordered. "Dispatch them as soon as possible to either this location, or the Widow's last known coordinates. I will know in an hour when they are closer to the ground."

"We will begin, Captain," the man said.

Iulianus cut the signal and looked over at his pilot. This man, Yanders Enick, had been with him from the beginning of this mad quest into the wilds.

"Lights off, but put us up high enough to see the native encampment from here," Iulianus ordered. He turned to the open door behind him. "All hands, prepare for maneuvering and possibly hostile insertion on the ground."

Iulianus opened a second line and pinged both women. He presumed that they would have turned the alarm sound off, but would set it to vibrate.

He mashed the button again, but still got no response. Finally, a hash of static came over the line, and he thought he could recognize Athanasia, but there were only tones, and not actual words. The stone must be blocking things.

He would have to get down there and warn her directly. And possibly rescue her, depending on how heavily armed the mutant raiders were, but the other locals on this planet seemed convinced that the deep desert dwellers were crazed killers. Iulianus would just have to make do.

Athanasia might have taken the more experienced combat troops, but the ones he had brought were not amateur hour.

Warbird-2 lifted with a smooth curve of power and Iulianus brought up the bow camera to show on this screen. This shuttle was unarmed, or he could have just strafed the natives into submission, most likely, but that was not an option now. Something to rectify at a later date, however.

If they were truly coming on a war footing, something had alerted them of interlopers in the temple complex. He wondered if the Widow's comm happened to be on the wrong frequency, or the mutants had a hidden scanner that had been listening.

Didn't matter now, as his shuttle got to altitude. The desert below them was flat enough and completely dark, with no moons overhead reflecting sunlight into the silver glow he had always taken for granted before. Now they only had diffraction from the sun itself, curling light around the edge of the atmosphere.

But he could see enough. T'Brask ground vehicles seemed to have a competition to see how many lights and how much candlepower they could string across the front of their vehicles for night driving.

He could see them crossing the desert along the one road they had into the old ruins. Dozens of them. They almost didn't appear to be moving, but that was the optical illusion of how far away they were. His professional eye said they were crossing the desert night at about sixty kph, which was impressive driving on unsurfaced roads at night in tight formations.

They would be onto the Widow's location in a matter of minutes, so he had to get there first.

"Put us down in the compound where the Widow went, and do it now," he ordered. "Then you'll lift clear and provide a communications relay for the other team when they arrive. If you can't reach me or the Widow, Rendakis is in command until I return."

"Yes, sir," Enick nodded as he brought the vessel around and poured on the engines to get them to the ruins quickly.

[23]
BAYJY

SHE TRIED to keep her heart beating at a normal pace, but that just so wasn't happening. Bayjy only had to look at the ship above her and everything got twitterpated all over again.

A real, live Urlan vessel. In mint condition, compared to what she was used to finding in the depths of space, exposed to solar wind and micrometeors. And maybe already stripped by someone else when nobody was looking.

She wondered who had designed this vessel. Urlan ships were usually big, ugly, and brutal, like all the rest of Urlan civilization. This almost felt like a fairy-tale ship by comparison. Like maybe Dad had bought his little princess a personal runabout for her and her friends to party in, and it had been able to carry her from wherever to Kryuome when the trouble started.

Right before the angry humans came out of warp and shattered the place.

She suppressed her fantasies and focused on why

it had been necessary to blow those bastards up, in spite of them occasionally creating art like this.

All a girl had to do was compare her bald purpleness to the hairy brown folks around her to understand what slavery had been like, back in the day. That little princess was probably served by a whole cast of underhumans who had no option to ever tell that little bitch **No**.

Stealing her ship, even two thousand years later, was justice. Princess had it coming.

Deep breath.

Rage and salvage are a bad combination. You end up missing something that kills you.

Bayjy glanced around to the four points of her mental compass, to make sure the others were all calm and prepared, with her at the center of the craziness.

An Urlan vessel, ready to fly away.

Just how rich did she want to be?

Bayjy pulled out both sensors and aimed them carefully at the hatch on the bottom of the bow. The ship had two pairs of landing legs behind her, and this chin rested just a half meter above the stone, so it was obvious how you got aboard.

Zero power indicators, but she wasn't surprised. Probably had gotten powered down here and stored out of the way for maintenance when all hell broke loose, and then princess wasn't going anywhere.

Just because of that asshole who built the rest of this place, she walked all the way around the ship's chin, scanning with all the patience in the world.

Nothing.

Okay, we can do this.

She approached the hatch and looked at it from

closer in. There was something painted on the right side, facing it. About eyeball level to Kyriaki, so about where an adult Urlan would put it.

Rualoh. In a fine, freehand script.

RU-ah-low. That was an Urlan name. Female. Classical antiquity, back maybe five thousand years ago when those bastards were just breaking out of their corner of space on the way to subjugating everyone else.

Princess Rualoh. Yeah, that sounded like the kind of woman who owned this thing, back in the day.

"Ship's name is *Princess Rualoh,*" Bayjy called to the others, just so they knew she wasn't goofing off here and trying to decide what to do with all that money when she got it. No, sirree.

She opened the little metal panel at Urlan height with a sharp thump, because it had jammed at some point, and studied the buttons. Standard ten-key with a couple of function buttons. Probably a security code to open the place, but she had no way to guess what Princess Rualoh might have chosen.

Didn't need to. She knelt and located the emergency panel at the bottom. That was standard on all Urlan vessels, by Imperial Law. Bayjy swapped out one scanner for the multi-tool and found a good prybar to pop it open.

Yup. Standard wheel. Same design as on *Longshot Hypothesis,* if you managed to disarm that sneaky secondary system Vee added that dropped bolts in anyway.

Some things hadn't changed in probably five thousand years. But hey, when you have something that works, you keep it until something better comes along, and nobody ever thinks about this kind of starship design except gearheads.

Another scan, because it was not possible to be too paranoid on this sort of thing, but the ship was dead as the princess who owned it.

Bayjy moved back from her squat and looked around.

"Big Guy, need your muscles here," she called.

The other three rearranged themselves as Dave came over, resting that stupid rocket launcher of his close at hand and studying the wheel in front of him, about the same circumference as his head.

"We use an Urlan design?" he asked with wonder in his voice as he studied the equipment.

"Everybody does, Big Guy," Bayjy replied with a smile. "Physics is physics."

"Huh," Dave nodded and put his hands on the wheel.

Bayjy rose and stepped back out of his way to watch the door itself. If it had been sealed all that time, the air would be bad by now. And maybe there was a dead princess just inside the hatch and she would fall out like a mummy and dust-splatter herself all over the place.

Bayjy pulled a cloth from a pocket and wrapped it around her mouth and nose as she thought about it.

Ya never know.

Big Guy got to work with those muscles. Had to bang on the wheel a few times, and then stand and kick it hard, but he got it broken free. After that, he knelt back down and worked his magic on it.

Bayjy studied the hatch as it finally started to move. Weirdly, it retracted straight up into the hull, rather than pivoting in, so there must not be an airlock here, just a mud room, or whatever the Urlan equivalent was.

Puff of gas as the seals finally broke, but she'd been expecting that, since the planet used to be lush and wet, and now was just all desert. Lower air pressure here, even underground.

Big Guy glanced at her and she nodded back, so he kept spinning that wheel. If it would open all the way, might as well do it now, so folks could walk in without having to crawl.

She shined a light into the space as it opened, getting down on her knees as well. Metal deck and walls inside, but that wasn't surprising. Princess Rualoh wouldn't want expensive rugs or carpeting down here for common spacers to track dirt and mud on.

Bad juju.

Nobody else made a sound, so she looked up. Backs of heads, so folks were keeping the corners protected and she could do her thing. Always a wonderful feeling, not to have that asshole Butler hanging over one shoulder and breathing that stinky breath on her skin.

Dave rolled the door up until he hit the stop at the top. The door was Urlan sized, so meter and a half wide and two and a half tall. Same external lights in this bay as everywhere else, from the glowstone, but she had to use a pocketflash to light the room up.

Soft colors, but badly faded, covered the walls. Probably more vibrant in ancient times, or maybe the Princess was just into pastels. Metal everywhere, including a spiral staircase on the right.

Seriously?

She stood up and walked clear out to the side to get a good view of this strange vessel.

Two decks ran front to back on that long axis with the engines tacked onto the outside. Her mud room was the deck below that, and Bayjy could see a wrap-around of glass or something that she took to be the flight deck, all the way across the front and halfway along the crest on each side. Call that fourth deck. At least three more above that, depending on how high the ceilings were. Actually a lot of living space for one or two people, if you got right down to it.

Fourth deck was the longest, front to back, not counting two and three that ran all the way to the back. If the exterior was fourteen meters wide, fourth deck looked to be about four times that long, so nearly sixty meters, with another eighty or so for the two below it, which she presumed would be where minions and servants had quarters and duty stations.

Somebody's got to keep the engines running, the air systems breathing, and the important people fed.

Hopefully, no dead Urlans stashed in there. Only one way to find out.

"Okay, folks," she announced. "This is where it gets interesting. I need one person inside with me, so Vee, you're up, since you understand starships better than anyone else right now. Big Guy, back to guard duty. Same with Glaxu. Kyrie, I want you at this hatch listening to us in case we need help. Questions?"

None. Hard professionals doing their thing, which happened to involve the potential for violence.

Vee walked close and studied the interior. The others were not starpilots and captains. Sure, Glaxu could fly, but he wasn't a mechanic. Vee had everything Bayjy needed in his head right now.

He also had a light in his off-hand, but no gun. Still, she'd seen him fast-draw the damned thing, so she wasn't worried. And the ship still didn't show a power signal when she scanned.

Museum piece, if they could somehow wrap a big enough transport sled around it to get it outside and build a shipping container large enough to haul it to space and slot it into a megafreighter.

"Urlan, huh?" Vee asked.

"Owner, yeah," Bayjy replied. "Don't know who designed it. Never seen anything like it, even in my research. And Urlan didn't do pretty like this."

She watched him step back and walk over to the same spot she had gone, in order to see the whole ship from a side. The swirls of a soft, almost wine-red mixed in with the steel gray. The two engine pods off to the sides of deck two, more square and simple grey without the prettier colors. That silly-ass-looking fin that stuck up like a dorsal fin a deck tall.

Bayjy wondered if maybe it was a gun turret of some sort. Or a docking fin you could use to drop a cargo box on, piggy-back.

Have to find the owner's manual at some point, just to see who had done this.

Unique starships were even better, because then you got bidding wars by men with more money than God, and egos to match.

Vee moved, and she fell into his shadow. She cut ships apart, but this one might actually fly, with a little TLC. Frightening, really.

Up the stairs and into the mud room.

"Spiral stairs?" he asked with a hint of disbelief.

"Our princess was weird," Bayjy replied. "But the other option was an elevator shaft top to bottom, I guess."

Two thousand years sealed was enough time for organics to evaporate into dust, but Vee walked to a side wall and tapped.

"Storage closets for suits and gear?" he turned to her.

"My theory is that crew were on decks two and three," Bayjy said. "Keep this stuff out of sight and we'll find a pretty bridge on four and personal quarters on five to seven."

"You leading or am I?" he grinned at her.

"Me first, dude," she chuckled. "You're just the hired help here."

He laughed back, and she saw some level of tension ease. His face was more relaxed in ways she really hadn't seen earlier. The shoulders came down. Valentinian became more himself.

Bayjy scanned the stairs themselves out of pure paranoid spite, but that stupid Urlan security designer had never been aboard this vessel, unless he was having a tumble with the little princess or something.

Bayjy started up the spiral, noting that the taller Urlan used stairs about five centimeters taller than the human species as a default. Not impossible, just kind of a pain in the ass.

She went up with her scanner out like a pistol, pinging anything and everything. Deck Two had a look like a kitchen towards the bow from what she could see down a wide hallway, and a heavy bulkhead with a hatch to the stern off the landing. Bayjy guessed that the Princess had crew through there when they weren't needed.

Out of sight and out of mind.

She ignored a pair of closed doors facing each other and moved to the bow with Vee staying far enough back to cover everything in event of trouble.

The archway opened into an industrial kitchen. The kind of place where your crew could easily cook dinner for a dozen gourmand Urlan. Those two chambers would be pantries filled with crap that had probably gone bad and maybe rancid. So not worth opening a door to get a fresh smell of dead skunk through the whole ship.

"You planning to rob a bank later?" Vee asked.

She turned to him blankly, blushed furiously, and pulled the cloth down around her neck now instead of obscuring half of her face.

How did that man know the exact buttons to embarrass her without ever coming across as mean?

"Maybe," she allowed after she got herself composed again. "Girl needs to have options."

He just nodded sagely. Vee was like that.

She could skip the rest for now, crew quarters wouldn't be all that interesting until they needed to access the engine room.

Up the stairs again.

Three looked like a salon and dining area, open with a big, wooden table that looked fragile with age now. Dry air and a good seal, plus nobody touching it for centuries, but anything might tip it over now, including the weight of dust slowly accumulating.

Instead of pantries, this room had a wet bar-looking thing at the front right, and a glass-fronted hutch with some gold-edged plates in there that might put all her eventual kids through college by themselves.

"So what's stuff like this worth?" Vee asked a little above a whisper.

"Just looting this room and getting that hutch's contents out you'd show a profit over the next few years, sitting on a beach somewhere," Bayjy whispered back.

"Yeah, I was afraid you were going to say that," Vee replied. "You supposed the Widow understands that? Or Butler told her?"

"If he did, she might be hunting us on this rock even now, Vee," Bayjy felt a cold hand of dread trace across the back of her neck slowly. "All the more reason to keep this quiet until we can get it all."

She watched him approach the hutch and stare at something, so she followed. All the fancy stuff a princess needed to have tea with all her lords and lady friends.

"Safe to open and take one thing as a prize to show the others?" he asked quietly.

She did her sorcery and dispelled any magical traps waiting them.

"You should be good."

Vee pulled the right half panel open and wrapped his hand around a tea mug with some sort of family coat of arms on it.

Oh, shit. That's probably Princess Rualoh's family symbol. We could actually figure out who she was with the right genealogical records.

Bayjy remembered to breathe as Vee wrapped the mug up in a cloth and stuffed it into the bag everyone was carrying with supplies.

"Treasure map, and treasure," he grinned. "What's above us?"

"Personal quarters and stuff," Bayjy guessed. "Let's find out."

Vee got to the stairwell and looked down.

"So far so good," he called to Kyrie, doing the thing Bayjy had forgotten in her lust and avarice.

"Same here," the babe yelled back up.

Up to fourth deck.

This was the bridge. No way in hell anything else made sense, with glass halfway around you. Two stations at the center for a captain and mate to fly the thing, and a lot of standing around room for guests to enjoy whatever view there was as you motored around.

Small office in back looked like where a captain could do paperwork away from the party, and opposite it was a bathroom for Urlan nobility.

Bayjy couldn't think of anyone else that required gold plate in order to piss more accurately.

Without power, nothing interesting on this deck except the view, so they yelled down to Kyrie and went up another one.

Guests apparently stayed on five. Four chambers, all open to sumptuousness, wrapped around a central area at the core with a big, round, semi-sunken lounge where you could stretch out and have fairly impressive orgies if you didn't want to make it to one of the bed chambers.

Bayjy tried not to roll her eyes at the thing, but failed.

Up to six, and her heart stopped. Just bounced once and then kind of fainted.

Princess read books. Lots of them. Eight shelving

units with ancient books carefully covered behind glass fronts that probably kept them sealed up and maybe even still legible today, depending on what she had printed them on.

Her feet betrayed her and she had a hand on a handle as soon as the scanner read safe.

Damned thing was locked, though. She'd be able to pick it later, but not being able to touch one just irritated the shit out of her right now.

Grumble.

Forward was a space Bayjy could only qualify as the Pretty Princess room. Rualoh was an artist, and an art lover, and had stuff in here, but it had aged badly. Watercolors on easels had more or less melted into rust with the easels themselves. She could probably untangle it all with patience and a magnet, once the rest of the ship was looted clean, but that was six months of effort she didn't need to do.

A piece of paper as fragile as onion skin rested atop a drawing table inclined about thirty degrees. Princess had been sketching a face with graphite. The pencil was still there, but rusty. The image was about half done. Female. Almost beautiful, even for an Urlan.

Bayjy had no idea if it was Rualoh, or one of her friends. And no way to check unless the electronic logs were recoverable and had images.

Crap, could the computer core still be intact after this long? In space, solar wind eventually got in and fried anything that wasn't hard-coded into plastic or something. Just a few ones and zeroes needed to flip and the data became garbage, but this was underground and covered with that glowstone, so there might not be any radiation down here, even after the electromagnetic pulses that would have eaten everything else on this planet.

Oh, wow.

What could she sell a genuine, Urlan navigational record system for? Enough to buy a planet somewhere and set herself up as queen?

Oh, the temptation. Vee, I'm gonna make you rich.

"One more?" Captain asked.

"One more," she agreed. "Kyrie, top deck and then we're headed back."

"Sounds good."

The Princess lived atop her tower. Simple as that.

Bayjy hadn't noticed how the aft end of this front fin tapered inward as you went up, but it was only about four meters wide now, while still fourteen across the bow. The stairwell came out right in the middle, with an even-more-amazing bathroom on one side, and an empty closet on the other.

Must have moved all her clothes and stuff to shore when the ship went into storage. Pity. Be nice to know how she dressed.

Overhead, the ceiling vaulted up to the rear from a low front, with two big skylights overhead.

"Huh," she muttered, wandering into the bedroom itself.

Sure enough, bed for six. More books. Dresser with a mirror and what looked like a makeup case that had evaporated over time. Cheap comb had survived longer than the ivory hair clips and pins Bayjy could see from their outlines in dust.

"What?" Vee asked from nearby.

"She laid there in bed," Bayjy pointed to the rotting pile of what looked like silk and wool. Then pointed at the ceiling. "She could watch the stars streak by in warpspace. Or have the captain flip the ship upside down relative to everyone else and watch a planet go by beneath her. Thinking the girl was an artist. Be nice to find a diary or something so we can know."

"Might be here," Vee shrugged. "Just got to look. That's why we were so careful breaking in. With enough water, we can stay down here for a week easy enough and maybe get this thing charged somehow to fly. Once we're away from the muties, all sorts of things become possible."

"You think it will fly?" she asked.

"Normally, this long on the ground and they fall over," Vee shrugged. "But we're in a controlled, sealed environment. Dry. Calm. Anything's possible. No idea how the engines or generators might work, but that's just physics, like you said. And if everyone else inherited Urlan tech after the war, then it should be something one of us can figure out."

"I'm giddy," she finally admitted to someone else.

"Me, too," he smiled. "Last several years have been one hustle after another, just to keep flying. I can't imagine a life where I could have luxury."

"Let's not screw this up, then," Bayjy laughed. "Time to roust the others and see what we do next."

Bayjy started down the stairs and heard a sound that didn't make any sense whatsoever, until Kyrie's voice floated up to them.

"Get your asses down here immediately," the woman yelled. "We got trouble."

[24]

ATHANASIA

"Damn it," Athanasia cursed, aware that all her men around her could hear.

None of them reacted, other than to perhaps look harder at the area around them.

After a fifteen-minute break to give her prey time to penetrate the catacombs, she had ordered the Force Leader to open up that thing.

Who put a trapdoor in the middle of a sidewalk? And how had Tarasicodissa managed to open the damned thing in the first place?

Three men had stayed back at that opening after she and the rest went ahead, to keep Dave Hall and his friends from somehow eluding her and escaping later. That still left her enough men to trap Tarasicodissa and the others, especially with the amount of explosives they had brought.

Why she might need to blow up a major office building had eluded Athanasia, but the men with her had the wherewithal to do it. Yes, she was dealing with killers.

But her comm stubbornly refused to connect. Palaiologos had tried to reach her, but something about the stone around them swallowed the signal and she got nothing but static.

Presumably, it was the same for him.

Did she continue on the trail, or withdraw to the surface where she could talk to Iulianus? Dividing her team even further at this point seemed insane, and she couldn't be in two places at once. Stephaneria was intelligent, but it was a bookish sort of thing, rather than a set of people skills.

But if Iulianus needed to talk to them, it must be important.

"Stephaneria, take one man and head back to the opening," Athanasia finally said, looking around this amazing shopping arcade they had wandered into, almost as well-lit as daytime outside and clean, however strange it was to find working lights in the ceiling. "Talk to Iulianus and then catch up with us."

Athanasia turned to the Force Leader and speared him with a hard, lethal promise of a slow death if he was wrong.

"That is where they went?" she nodded in the direction of what looked to be a secret portal slightly ajar on one wall.

Stephaneria nodded and grabbed a trooper, but Athanasia held her arm for a second.

The Force Leader understood the tightrope he was walking, but nodded.

"They may have gone other places, ma'am," he said gruffly. "But that looks the most obvious, if they don't know we're behind them, and we can always stage out of this room."

"Go," Athanasia turned to Stephaneria. "There will be someone here when you get back."

The librarian drew her own pistol now and departed back up that long, sinuous tunnel that would take her to the surface and whatever other problems might have arisen.

Athanasia looked around and counted noses. Five people at the entrance left her with six troopers plus herself. Not enough to take on the other group, if the eye witness accounts were to be believed.

And she had been married to Dave Hall for thirty years, so she knew exactly how dangerous that man was. Not that she could convey something like that to these mere killers.

But she drew her own pistol and nodded to the man she was relying on now, the Force Leader whose name she hadn't even bothered to learn before this. Not one she would need to take into her bed to bind him to her eventual throne, but someone she might need to promote to a bodyguard position, if he retained his current level of competence.

The Force Leader nodded back and tapped two men to approach the door, with the other three behind her.

As with the trapdoor, this was a single cut of granite, polished and tiled on one side, and rough the rest of the way. It opened with a fingertip, so the pin must be as smooth as glass, even after all this time, but the rest of the facility had impressed her equally.

Whatever else you might want to say about the Urlans, they built to last.

Another tunnel was revealed, curving away as she looked inside. Another weird design aesthetic, but the underground arcade around her did not have a single flat wall visible, so perhaps they just liked to move like snakes underground.

They entered now, moving as quiet as ghosts around the curve.

Another door was ajar at the far end of the hallway, but the two men on point had frozen well back from it, kneeling tight against the walls and peering ahead.

The acoustics were horrible, so she could not understand the words, but a female voice was yelling something in that room just ahead of them.

Given the head start, the other group had stopped here. Or found the treasure that had drawn everyone across so much distance.

Athanasia wondered if she might just kill them all and loot the place herself. If there was value here, she could use it to expand her army and her fleet. Good piracy required constant funds, which was why most folks settled for smuggling instead, where the rest of the job might pay for itself and the risks were much lower.

One of the scouts oozed backwards like a glacier until he was out of sight from the door. He gestured them to move backwards as well, so the team was out of hearing from whoever was up there.

"Large room beyond that door," the man whispered quietly. "Major vaulted ceiling. Space goes on forever. Like they had the whole courtyard above us, and then built a city atop that, with a stadium down here."

"Tarasicodissa?" she asked the man.

They all knew why they were here. Pictures of their prey had been circulated and memorized.

"Unseen, Commander," he said. "We froze when

we saw anything beyond the door, and I don't think that anyone saw us."

"How do we know?" she demanded quietly.

"We don't," the Force Leader spoke up. "If they did, they would remain quiet while setting an ambush for us, same as we're doing for them."

"We know at least two of them are in that room, from the voices. One male, one female," the scout added.

"I suggest we move most of the team back and keep the two scouts up here as a tripwire, Commander," the Force Leader said. "We can go get the rest if we need to, with them hopefully bottled up in the room beyond us for now. Also, until we know what message Captain Palaiologos has for us, we should wait. It could be more trouble."

"I agree," Athanasia said.

She moved backwards as the others did, back almost as far as the hidden door that had allowed them into this tunnel. Athanasia didn't remember any other doors on this side of the arcade that might represent other exits Tarasicodissa might take, but she didn't know how big that chamber was, so there must be other ways out.

Athanasia didn't like it, but there wasn't much she could do right now.

Hopefully, Stephaneria would have the information she needed shortly.

THE MAN that accompanied her was just another of
the killers Stephaneria had come to realize were her
future. Athanasia would need such men to form a
middle tier of the social structure the Widow would
be building.

Stephaneria felt like a princess, but she also
understood that Athanasia was grooming her to have
children after all, perhaps, and help form a ruling
family for this new thing.

She wondered if that would be enough to keep
her interested, after she had killed Tarasicodissa.
Everything else truly paled by comparison to that.

"Stephaneria Meers-Bolat approaching," she
called when she thought she was close enough for
the guards ahead to understand her voice. "Code
word mongoose."

"Acknowledge mongoose," a voice replied.
"Code word upright."

Good, these were her men. Well, Athanasia's men,

but they considered her an extension of the Widow, and bowed to her automatically.

"Status, ma'am?" the one closest asked as she came around the corner into the face of three guns.

"Messages from the top are being hashed by static," Stephaneria said, falling into the coldly descriptive vocabulary of the soldier in the field. Just the minimum, as tightly packed verbally as possible. "Open the hatch carefully. Expect a shuttle and friendly troops on the outside, perhaps."

"Ambush potential?"

"Unknown," she replied, pointing her pistol loosely in the direction that the night sky would open into.

The others did the same as the man at the rear opened the trapdoor silently just enough to peek out in all directions before opening it the rest of the way.

Stephaneria heard sounds on the outside and saw lights moving around.

She pulled her comm and keyed the button.

"Palaiologos," she called simply. "I've surfaced. Does this channel work?"

"It does," he came back immediately. "We have significant trouble. Something has awakened the T'Brask locals and the entire tribe appears to be headed this way at high speed. They will arrive within minutes. Are you prepared for evacuation?"

"No," Stephaneria growled. "Athanasia sent me to the opening to communicate with you while she pursued Tarasicodissa's party deeper into the catacombs. Our comms do not work underground for reasons I have not determined."

There was a moment of silence. Stephaneria

climbed up next to the guard and saw *Warbird-2* parked not far away, with more troopers pouring out of the aft ramp. She flashed a light at them and saw Palaiologos leading them across the sand. Quickly, he was close enough to talk, but the shuttle's screaming engines overrode everything, so no conversation was possible.

The man grabbed her and pulled her ear to his mouth.

"We have to get Athanasia out of the tunnels," he yelled.

She started to argue with the man, but the troopers with him suddenly dropped to knees or flat on the sand and opened fire on the far end of the long courtyard.

Worse, fire came hosing back, just as quickly, if not as well armed. There was no time to engage in a firefight here, as Athanasia would be engaging Tarasicodissa at the other end and they would all be trapped shortly. All the locals had to do was circle like sharks and Stephaneria would never be able to escape.

She grabbed Palaiologos by the arm and pulled him down the stairs.

"Can we hole up there?" she asked.

"Not a chance," he said grimly. "Probably one hundred gunmen with armed vehicles immediately, plus whatever friendlies they have called in from other tribes."

Stephaneria grimaced and turned to the others.

"Attack on the surface," she called to her four men. "Stand back and prepare for the rest of the friendly team into the tunnels."

She let the captain see the situation. This room, and the space and the tunnel that exited. He nodded and climbed back up the surface.

She heard him yell for his men, and then return, followed by others pelting madly down the stairs. She counted eleven total, so enough to kill Valentinian, but not enough to take on mutants. Certainly not the kind the planetary locals had described.

"We can close the trapdoor," she said as the sound of weapon fire faded somewhat. "I am not sure if we can lock it from this side. We might be able to collapse it with explosives."

"Would we be trapped down here?" he asked.

"We have discovered extensive tunnels," Stephaneria replied. "What I don't know is if the locals are aware of them enough to enter by another path and attack us underground."

Palaiologos looked around and up at the two men who had stopped at the top and continued to fire at anything that moved. Return fire was growing more accurate.

How much explosives did the T'Brask have? Or missiles they might use?

One of the gunmen died suddenly, pitching backwards with a smoking hole in his chest large enough for her fist.

"Seal it up," Palaiologos ordered.

The gunmen around her suddenly got serious and quiet. Two of hers and one of the others immediately directed her to move back down the tunnel out of the way. Protecting her, she presumed. She left one of hers here and took the other two with her all the way back to the big room Athanasia had found earlier.

Across the big chamber, she saw another of the friendly gunmen standing just outside the apparently-secret door that Tarasicodissa had found earlier. Stephaneria left one man at this first door and took Palaiologos's gunman with her across the space. Back up the hallway she could hear the sounds of running feet coming towards her, so she also began to jog. The man watching had his gun up.

"Friendlies," she yelled. "But the mutants are attacking the mouth of the tunnel and Captain Palaiologos is going to blow it shut."

Athanasia was suddenly there as Stephaneria jogged closer. Several of her men emerged, but she turned to one and the man pressed the trapdoor mostly closed.

"What's happening?" Athanasia demanded in a quiet voice.

"Iulianus is behind me with his team," Stephaneria said. "The T'Brask were just beginning an attack on the trapdoor with overwhelming forces, so he ordered them to blow the tunnel in and is coming this way."

"How do we get out?" Athanasia asked.

"We look for another secret tunnel," Stephaneria replied gravely. "Presumably they exist. At some point, either we can escape the T'Brask, or they will enter the catacombs and engage us."

The noise of men running brought Stephaneria's head around. Captain Palaiologos led them at a jog until they suddenly slowed in wonder as they entered an underground stadium, for lack of a better term.

"Hold this point," he turned and ordered the men

around him. "Close the door but stay out of the direct line until the overpressure clears."

He turned immediately and jogged across the space.

"Have you found them?" he asked as he got close.

"They are beyond this door and another tunnel," Athanasia replied. "What happened on the surface?"

"The entire mutant tribe from the village suddenly all leapt into vehicles and began to race across the surface at high-speed," Palaiologos said angrily, showing rare emotion. He was more interesting when he was acting like a pirate, rather than the bland bureaucrat he had been impersonating for so long. "I could not reach you in time for you to escape the tunnels, so I came down."

"And trapped yourself with me," Athanasia pointed out acidly.

"Should I have left you instead?" he fired right back. "They would have fallen on you like a pack of wolves."

"And this is better?" she sneered.

"You have twice as many men now, and warning," he said simply. "Plus…"

Whatever he was going to say was drowned in a tremendous earthquake that shook the entire universe. Across the arcade, Stephaneria watched the door simply explode off its hinges, flying a dozen meters before it stopped skidding.

Immediately after the sound subsided, she watched a handful of men go back into the tunnel at a jog, while the rest found spots behind pillars and in dry water fountains with their weapons covering all directions against the next attack.

"The trapdoor is hopefully sealed now," Captain

Palaiologos said simply. "We have time to find another way out, rather than having the natives come pouring down that tunnel at us. I suggest we use it. Both shuttles are close enough to rescue us, once we find a safe landing zone for them."

"Tarasicodissa will have heard that," Athanasia said.

"And he's as trapped as we are right now," Iulianus snapped. "The locals will not grant him a free pass to escape."

"What would you suggest, then?" Stephaneria knew the tone of her voice could have curdled milk, but she saw where the man was going. Feared it. Snarled inwardly at the possible necessity.

"We should talk to the man," Iulianus replied simply. "His presence prevents us from exploring the rest of these catacombs safely. At least as safely as possible with mutant incursions likely. But he also has no transport handy that can safely get him away from the locals."

"Work with him?" Stephaneria felt rage take hold of her soul.

Ugly, bloody hatred. That she could need the very man she had crossed so many light-years to kill. That he might be close enough to kiss and still denied to her because of his other two doxies.

She felt her fist clenching around the grip of her pistol, so she holstered it before she fired a shot in anger.

"Work with him," Captain Palaiologos replied. "At least for now. Only fools fight in a burning house, ladies. And this house is on fire."

"You handle negotiations, then, Captain,"

Athanasia said in a voice almost as dark and ugly as Stephaneria's felt.

But then, that woman had pursued Dave Hall even further. And been married to him, a spouse abandoned when he had a midlife crisis. Unlike Strauss, Hall hadn't even had a bimbo as an excuse.

"Truce until we escape this situation," the Widow continued. "I will honor that much."

Captain Palaiologos bowed at the waist and stepped past them abruptly. The one gunman opened the tunnel as the captain approached. Stephaneria fell into Athanasia's wake as they followed. The second tunnel was much shorter than the first, and quickly enough they came to the spot where the two scouts were holding vigil.

"Not safe past here, sir," the Force Leader whispered as they did.

"Good enough," Palaiologos replied, taking the pistol out of his holster and handing it to Stephaneria with a hard look.

He knew how deadly she was. He was trusting her to watch his back, rather than Athanasia.

Maybe he was worth more than just keeping around and alive as a possible sperm donor for Athanasia's plans, after all.

Iulianus Palaiologos stepped just past the men and took a deep breath.

"Valentinian Tarasicodissa," he bellowed in a command voice taught by the *Gymnasia Dominia*, she presumed. "This is Iulianus Palaiologos. We need to talk. I would like to step out into the open. I am unarmed, but have a large group of troops hidden behind me."

Stephaneria was aghast at the utter audacity of

the thing. Walk right up and demand to parley? With that scum Tarasicodissa?

"Are you alone?" Valentinian called back.

She knew that voice. Dreamed about it. Hated it. Loved it. Wanted to see him again. Wanted to run her hands through his hair. Wanted to kill him.

Maybe she would get her chance yet.

[26]

VALENTINIAN

VALENTINIAN MOVED QUICKLY. Kyriaki wasn't one to panic, so bad things must be brewing. He politely shifted Bayjy out of his way and raced down that stupid, spiraling staircase until he was at the lowest deck and facing outward.

The air was dusty and quiet as he scanned things, so he slowed down and drew his pistol.

It finally registered what the sound was he had heard. This planet might have earthquakes still, a leftover of the bombardment, but he had always heard that those were long, rumbly things. This had been a sharp spike.

Like an explosion somewhere close enough to be transmitted through the ground.

He peeked out enough to locate Kyriaki and Dave, but they were suddenly hidden behind some of the large, unidentified equipment in this hangar bay, guns pointed at the door back the way they had come.

"Valentinian Tarasicodissa," a voice filled with

authority suddenly called out. A man's voice. One he didn't recognize immediately, but the tone was like coming home. "This is Iulianus Palaiologos. We need to talk. I would like to step out into the open. I am unarmed, but have a large group of troops hidden behind me."

He recognized the name from Bohrne Station and Glaxu's stories of Chatosig. Iulianus Palaiologos, former captain of *Dominion-427* turned pirate and now the man commanding the old M'Rai cruiser *Phoenix*.

A brother officer, in another timeline.

"Are you alone?" Valentinian stuck his head out the hatch of *Princess Rualoh* far enough to see a shadow in the middle distance up that tunnel.

"I am presently," the man said simply, confidently.

"Hands open where I can see them," Valentinian focused his voice. "Move slowly and politely, so nobody has to kill you accidentally."

Glaxu was nowhere to be seen, but that was fine. That killer was three dimensional in combat as well as mindset. He would likely be above them somewhere, waiting to pounce like a big cat.

Bayjy was pounding down the stairs behind him, and would add her plasma rifle shortly. There weren't many weapons more fun to use on a packed hallway than a plasma rifle, at least if you wanted survivors. Detonators also had their place.

And he still had a pair of detonators handy, and could probably nail that doorway from here with one of them if pushed.

Palaiologos stepped into view and paused at the threshold. He was dressed in a piratical version of his old Dominion uniform. Tall boots in rough black leather. Jodhpur pants in dark gray tucked in at the knee. Long black tunic with a red sash tied around it instead of the simple leather belt. Maybe over it, since Valentinian could see an empty holster.

The face was the same as a thousand others just like him from the Dominion Armada. Bland in ways that were hard to categorize, except there was a fire in his eyes that line officers rarely had.

Pirates, maybe.

"Closer," Valentinian went ahead and pointed his pistol at the man, sure that Kyriaki was prepared to fire on the doorway the moment that anything twitched.

What Dave could do in close quarters was its own level of frightening.

Captain Palaiologos stepped deeper into the big room with great deliberation. Nobody was likely to grab him, as they had all taken up spots well away from the door, on this side across the open space of the hangar, but that man would be dead before he took a third step running right now, any way you wanted to look at it.

"Did you just blow up the entry tunnel?" Valentinian hazarded a guess at the man. "With you and yours trapped inside?"

"I did," Palaiologos replied with a nod. "Time was critical and the threat extreme."

"Why's that?" Valentinian asked.

"Something alerted the mutants outside to your presence," the former Dominion Officer said. "The entire tribe was closing on the ruins and had called for others to help. I got here just fast enough to alert the Widow, who was in the catacombs stalking you.

The attackers were at the tunnel entrance. What you heard came from the booby trap we left behind. I'm not sure how many of them died, but the survivors will exercise more caution in the future."

"And the tunnel is sealed?" Valentinian looked at the man with at least a greater respect for his pure, lethal professionalism.

Yes, Dominion Armada Captain. Some of the best navy men in the galaxy, because that was the least forgiving place you could serve.

"I presume so," the captain nodded back. "Part of my ground force is checking, and most of them are arrayed defensively in that major arcade back there against further attacks and flank movements."

"So why are you here, Captain?" Valentinian stared at him across the large room.

"I would like to propose a truce of common cause, Captain Tarasicodissa," Palaiologos replied. "Everyone is trapped down here for now, so if we do not work together, we will do the job for the mutants. Plus, I have shuttles that can remove people from the surface quickly, if we can find an exit, so I will offer you safe transport to your ship as trade, and a head start off the surface of the planet. On my honor as a Dominion Armada officer."

"You aren't one anymore, Captain Palaiologos," Valentinian fired back at the man.

At the pirate.

"Nor are you, Captain Tarasicodissa," the pirate captain replied in deadly seriousness. "That doesn't change anything."

Valentinian was surprised. It was a good offer, if it turned out to be legitimate. And Palaiologos had known Butler Vidy-Wooders. Knew what reputations really meant after the man had forever burned his own character, a story Valentinian and his crew had helped spread across all of Wildspace to pay the man back.

Could Valentinian trust this son of a bitch to keep his word?

"Are the Widow and the Librarian with you?" he asked sharply.

"They are," the man agreed. "Back up that tunnel safely. She has placed me in charge of negotiating a truce that will get us all out of here alive, if possible."

So, Captain Palaiologos. Willing to put your entire reputation for honor and honesty on the line right now? Especially with two women than have chased Dave and I all the way across Wildspace? And chased Dave and Kyriaki clear from the Dominion?

"Walk slowly back through that door and close it behind you," Valentinian ordered. "In ten minutes, knock loudly, count to five, and then open it for my answer. I promise you will be safe until we talk again."

Palaiologos studied him across the fifty meters of space, at least as well as possible, with Valentinian mostly hidden except for his face and his gun arm.

Calculating the odds.

Finally he nodded. Bowed at the waist, even, like they were back on Cronos Prime and still wearing the black and gray of the Dominion Armada.

"Until then, Captain Tarasicodissa," he said simply, pivoting on a heel and walking slowly to the door like there weren't guns ready to splatter him everywhere at the slightest mistake.

He closed that door and Valentinian let go a breath.

Kyriaki exploded from cover and crossed the space to the door in the blink of an eye, dragging a large something against the door itself. It looked heavy, and would probably keep someone from kicking the door open to start an ambush from their end.

Valentinian moved out of the old ship and towards a workbench that looked solid enough for engine parts to rest atop, and capable of stopping a heavy flamer for a while. Bayjy was right behind him.

Dave appeared from a nearby corner like the greatest magic trick in the world. He approached silently, with a deadly serious look on his face. Glaxu came down from a nearby catwalk. Bayjy exited the ship on silent feet.

"Okay, I've bought us time," Valentinian said. "What the hell do we do now?"

[27]
DAVE

NEVER IN HIS wildest nightmares had Dave envisioned a situation remotely like this one. Trapped underground on a strange, alien world, with his friends along for the terror, being chased by Athanasia and her whole crew of piratical misfits and deserters.

Although he wasn't sure he could call them deserters, even in his former role as the Dominator. Someone had most likely given Palaiologos specific orders to serve Athanasia's needs and keep her away from the Dominion. Possibly for the rest of her life. Or his own.

What would it do to a man like Palaiologos to be ordered to throw away your entire life and spend it so far from home?

Obviously, they had chosen well, to find a man willing to live those commandments to this extent.

Did he dare trust the man not to kill him? To keep Athanasia and Stephaneria from killing him and Valentinian and Kyriaki?

To let the former Dominator just get away?

It all came down to that, didn't it? The very Gods of Creation must be laughing right now as they maneuvered all the players onto a single board for the first time and put them all in a larger trap.

Dave walked over to where Vee and the others had drifted a little closer together. Kyriaki was watching the main door like a mama bear with a sleeping cub. Glaxu had the left flank. Dave moved so he could handle the right, that long tunnel that his brain kept wanting to interpret as the flight tube for this strange, little ship they were sheltering beneath.

"Do we run or do we chance it?" Valentinian looked up at him and asked earnestly.

It dawned on Dave just how young the man was. He tended to forget that Vee was only about twenty-four, as he carried himself so much older, most of the time. Kyriaki was the same way, having lived a monastic existence for most of her adult life.

Only he and Bayjy had truly been out in the bad stuff, knee deep in mud and elbow deep in gore.

Plus, it was his life that the rest were truly after. Vee and Kyriaki were just accessories after the crime that was Dave Hall.

"Like he said, Vee," Dave finally spoke. "They have surface transport and I'm pretty sure your truck will be toast as soon as the muties realize that we must have a camp around here somewhere and go looking for it. Without that, it's a two- or three-day walk to the ship. Through hostile territory."

"Any chance we could kill enough of those bastards that the rest will leave us alone?" Bayjy asked.

She wasn't usually the bloodthirsty one, but

Basuk had warned them what would happen to any women captured by the T'Brask.

Fates worse than death.

"I doubt it," Dave smiled grimly at her. "Palaiologos said they had put out the call for the other tribes to come help. If this takes on religious connotations, us down here in the ruins, we may be facing the entire species after a bit."

"We can try," Kyriaki promised the other woman in a deadly tone.

Bayjy nodded in a conspiracy that would carry them far beyond the deaths of all the men around them.

Dave would certainly go down fighting, if it came to that.

But time was burning the candle.

"Either we have to take the man at his word, or we just open fire with everything we have, like at Truqtok's palace, and hope for the best," Dave said simply.

"Truqtok had it coming," Vee growled. "And I promised him he would be safe for ten minutes. I am not interested in burning my reputation, either. Without honor, we are all as nothing."

Dave recognized one of the phrases pounded relentlessly into young minds as the Dominion Armada shaped them into warriors. Vee and Palaiologos were going to approach this like Armada officers. He was just the first mate on a tramp freighter trying to make an honest Solar.

And if you believed that, I've got a used speeder bike to sell you.

"We have several minutes, if we hurry," Glaxu's voice floated down from above them. "Should we explore this tunnel and see if it will shelter us or provide escape from the tunnels?"

Vee shook himself and looked around, transforming himself suddenly as Dave watched, into a general planning a campaign again, rather than a kid in over his head and trying to save everyone from their own bad decisions.

"Yes," he ordered. "Glaxu, make a high-speed run down this long tunnel and see if it emerges into any place we can use. I'm willing to engage in a running firefight with the locals, especially if the others are with us, if this will get us to the surface."

Valentinian looked back over his shoulder at the ship as Glaxu pelted madly down an overhead catwalk.

"Bayjy, can this thing fly?" he asked simply. "I don't even need space. Just enough to get us to *Longshot* or even out of the city where the Widow's shuttles might meet us for dust off."

"Lemme look, Vee," she said, racing back to the hatch and disappearing from Dave's view.

"You two, don't go far, but explore other corners and see if there are doors out or in," Vee said. "I'll hold this space until he comes back, and give the rest of you warning if something goes sideways."

Dave started to say something, but the kid was *on*, and anything at this point might just knock him off that fine, perfect edge a captain needed to thread his ship through danger. Instead, Dave put his long legs to use, jogging towards a set of offices.

The architect he could have become in another world recognized this as a secret base inside a secret base, so Dave didn't think that there would be another direct chamber from that underground shopping space to here, but mechanics and staff would need to come and go, so there must be something.

He regretted that the Urlan didn't believe in laws regarding fire hazards, or someone would have put up evacuation maps on the walls regularly and he could pull one down to navigate by.

There would be nothing more lethal than for a large group of humans and allies to be moving blindly through these tunnels, and run smack dab into a pack of muties. Too many people would die before things got untangled, and he and his friends would have to slaughter everyone to make sure they could escape quietly.

Sure enough, he found what his brain interpreted as a fire door, located at the end of a short hallway that led him past several offices where foremen and managers might have once done their business.

He didn't open it, obeying Bayjy's strict orders on such a thing, because he would have been willing to bet a good chunk of cash on this one being armed and lethal somehow, even two thousand years later.

Letting Athanasia go through, while tempting, would probably just get the rest of the group killed as well.

Still, it was enough for now. Likely, the others had run into similar semi-dead ends as well, but these sorts of things would give them all options to escape from this death trap in good order.

He would need to run. They all would. Deeper into Wildspace, possibly exiting the zone altogether and finding out what the other five sides offered in the way of freedom from his ex-wife.

Vee might even have to do the unthinkable and

part with *Longshot Hypothesis*, just because that ship would stay in folks' memories long after they had flown away, giving Athanasia a trail she could follow.

He did not doubt for a second that a head start was all she would be willing to honor.

Every day for the rest of his life looking over his shoulder. Waiting for the axe to fall.

He made his way back to the place where Vee was hiding, gun drawn and holding the rear flank in case the others had attacked and Dave needed to flee.

Dave didn't think he deserved the sort of friendship Valentinian Tarasicodissa was offering, but the man had claimed Dave as one of his own, so Dave would count him the same way.

Kyriaki and Bayjy were just two more. Even Glaxu had joined the family.

Now they just had to make it out of here alive.

Kyriaki was back as well, grim as ever, but he could see hope in her eyes, so maybe she had also found exits they could use. Bayjy emerged, as if she had the same countdown timer flashing before her.

Even Glaxu came towards them like a racing locomotive.

"If I had a month and access to *Longshot* for fuel and stuff, maybe," Bayjy began simply. "They put her to bed clean enough, but it's still been a long time down. She's definitely not Urlan on the outside, but those engines are, so pretty standard."

"Okay, it was, as we like to play them around here, a longshot hypothesis anyway," Vee chuckled and the others joined in nervously, Dave included. "If it was just us and the Widow, I'd maybe study out how to do it, but right now we consider this ship a complete loss and walk away, understood?"

Dave wasn't surprised at the fire in those eyes now. This was the Valentinian Tarasicodissa he had picked out of five thousand names when a middle-aged Dominator decided he needed a new life. Luck, honor, and grit.

"But…" Bayjy started to say, but Vee cut her off.

"We are done, Bayjy," he said harshly. "If we look back now, try to circle back later, this ship will get us killed. I can't imagine the T'Brask won't find a way down these tunnels. Probably they're already coming from the direction of the stage once they figure everything out. They'll find it and us if we're still here. I'd rather be poor and gone, instead of trying to get rich off a princess's corpse, however beautiful Sleeping Beauty might be. *There will be other ships.*"

Dave could tell she wanted to grumble, but swallowed it. Valentinian was right, simple as that. They had a very high chance of dying in these tunnels if they got distracted, with or without the muties.

He had no idea how his wife would take the news when she arrived.

"Glaxu?" Vee turned to the speedster now.

"This is a launch and landing tunnel, Captain," the Mondi chirped happily. "I was able to go a distance of four kilometers in a straight line and return, without finding the far end, so I presume another park or perhaps an artificially-hollow building on the mountain side of the city."

Four kilometers? Yes, Dave supposed that at over thirty kph, he could have done that and gotten back in the time allowed.

Dave had never been a sprinter, but he could still outrun everyone else here over a hundred kilometer march. Maybe even a Mondi, depending on how much endurance the species had.

"Okay, time's just about up," Vee said, squaring his shoulders. "Everybody move to my left and find a space to hide over there, in case we need to retreat down that long tunnel to escape from whoever comes. If Glaxu's nose is right, it also takes us farther away from the stage where I expect trouble to originate. Questions?"

There were none. It was do or die time. Forlorn hope.

Except that Dave looked inside himself and still found hope. It was a strange thing, but he just knew that Vee's luck would hold and they would find a way out of here.

Now he just had to survive a reunion with the woman who had once been the love of his life.

Dave moved to cover and took stock. He had the cannon that could shoot down low-flying aircraft, plus two pistols. He drew the heavy flamer after slinging the rifle and held it loosely in case he needed it.

They would be too far away for swords, unless things got completely out of hand. And Athanasia was pretty good with a blade herself.

As he settled, someone rapped loudly at that door.

Dave sighted his flamer on the space and waited. If it was an attack, the impact of a heavy flamer bolt would go through the door at this range, and then shatter a nice chunk of the wood into shrapnel that would pelt other survivors in the tunnel while his friends started killing people.

A pause, and the door opened.

Captain Palaiologos stood in the door, still calm and unarmed. Dave was too far off to one side to see anybody behind him, but he suspected the man had put everyone back in the main chamber for now, reducing the temptation for mischief on anybody's part.

"Captain Tarasicodissa?" the pirate captain asked.

Vee rose from cover and stepped out into the open, holstering his pistol and relying on his friends.

"Captain Palaiologos," Valentinian replied. "We will accept your truce with one additional note. After our escape from this space, I had promised the merchants of Meeredge the story of what we found here, in trade for their original assistance, so we will all fly there directly and share the tale with them. After that, everyone will be able to depart in peace. Do you find this satisfactory?"

The man paused for a moment, processing such a strange addendum. Finally he nodded.

"Yes," Palaiologos said gravely. "All such promises should be honored, if we wish to remind the rest of the galaxy that we are civilized beings. I accept."

He turned without moving and faced the doorway.

"Athanasia, it is done," he called back up the hallway. "Would you care to join us?"

Dave held his breath. His heartrate was going as fast as a blundering seventeen-year-old who had just laid eyes on this beautiful creature four years his elder, and decided then and there that he would win her heart.

Had it really been thirty-five years? And still she did these things to him.

She emerged from the tunnel, proud and strong as ever, a pistol in her holster and a sword pommel peeking over one shoulder. Her hair hadn't lost any luster, but it was fading from spun gold into clouds racing overhead. Her hourglass body was still sleek and deadly as ever.

She looked around and found him almost instantly, even crouched down.

A spark of lightning passed between them, just like it once had, oh so long ago.

Dave rose, dropping his flamer back into the holster.

The Librarian from Bohrne Station had also emerged, but she was a faint shadow aftereffect as Dave began to walk forward.

Absently, he noted that whatever other men had accompanied his wife, they had stayed up in the tunnel for now, just as Kyriaki, Bayjy, and Glaxu were remaining under cover.

Quickly enough, Dave took his place at Valentinian's side, across from Athanasia, herself flanked by the other two.

She stared up at him with an inscrutable face, still as lovely as ever, even as age had finally begun to lay claim to it. If she was going to kill him, she would do it now, but he didn't see his death in her eyes.

Not yet, anyway.

It wasn't lurking very deep.

Dave smiled at Athanasia.

"Hello, my love," he said simply.

Blaze Ward writes science fiction in the Alexandria Station universe (Jessica Keller, The Science Officer, The Story Road, etc.) as well as several other science fiction universes, such as Star Dragon, the Collective, and more. He also writes odd bits of high fantasy with swords and orcs. In addition, he is the Editor and Publisher of *Boundary Shock Quarterly Magazine*. You can find out more at his website www.blazeward.com, as well as Facebook, Goodreads, and other places.

Blaze's works are available as ebooks, paper, and audio, and can be found at a variety of online vendors. His newsletter comes out regularly, and you can also follow his blog on his website. He really enjoys interacting with fans, and looks forward to any and all questions—even ones about his books!

Never miss a release!
If you'd like to be notified of new releases, sign up for my newsletter.

I will never spam you or use your email for nefarious purposes. You can also unsubscribe at any time.

http://www.blazeward.com/newsletter/

Connect with Blaze!

Web: www.blazeward.com
Boundary Shock Quarterly (BSQ):
https://www.boundaryshockquarterly.com/

facebook.com/KRPBlaze

goodreads.com/Blaze_Ward

bookbub.com/authors/blaze-ward

Knotted Road Press fiction specializes in dynamic writing set in mysterious, exotic locations.

Knotted Road Press non-fiction publishes autobiographies, business books, cookbooks, and how-to books with unique voices.

Knotted Road Press creates DRM-free ebooks as well as high-quality print books for readers around the world.

With authors in a variety of genres including literary, poetry, mystery, fantasy, and science fiction, Knotted Road Press has something for everyone.

Knotted Road Press
www.KnottedRoadPress.com